SERIES PRAISE ᵧₒᵣ BARRY FORBES

AMAZING BOOK! My daughter is in 6th grade and she is home-schooled, she really enjoyed reading this book. Highly recommend to middle schoolers. *Rubi Pizarro on Amazon*

I have three boys 11-15 and finding a book they all like is some-times a challenge. This series is great! My 15-year-old said, "I actu-ally like it better than Hardy Boys because it tells me currents laws about technology that I didn't know." My reluctant 13-year-old picked it up without any prodding and that's not an easy feat. *Shantelshomeschool on Instagram*

I stumbled across the author and his series on Instagram and had to order the first book! Fun characters, good storyline too, easy read-ing. Best for ages 11 and up. *AZmommy2011 on Amazon*

Virtues of kindness, leadership, compassion, responsibility, loyalty, courage, diligence, perseverance, loyalty and service are character-ized throughout the book. *Lynn G. on Amazon*

Barry, he LOVED it! My son is almost 14 and enjoys reading but most books are historical fiction or non-fiction. He carried your book everywhere, reading in any spare moments. He can't wait for book 2 – I'm ordering today and book 3 for his birthday. *Ourlifeathome on Instagram*

Perfect series for our 7th grader! I'm thrilled to have come across this perfect series for my 13-year old son this summer. We purchased the entire set! They are easy, but captivating reads and he is enjoying them very much. *Amylcarney on Amazon*

THE TREASURE OF SKULL VALLEY

A MYSTERY SEARCHERS BOOK

BARRY FORBES

THE TREASURE OF SKULL VALLEY

A MYSTERY SEARCHERS BOOK

VOLUME 5

By
BARRY FORBES

ST. LEO PRESS

DISCLAIMER

Prescott, the former capital of the Arizona Territory, is considered by many to be the state's crown jewel. Aside from this central Arizona locale, *The Mystery Searchers* series is a work of fiction. Names, characters, businesses, places, events, incidents, and other locales are either the products of the author's imagination or used in a fictitious manner. Any resemblance to actual persons, living or dead, or actual events is purely coincidental.

Read more at www.MysterySearchers.com

For Linda,
whose steadfast love and encouragement
made this series possible

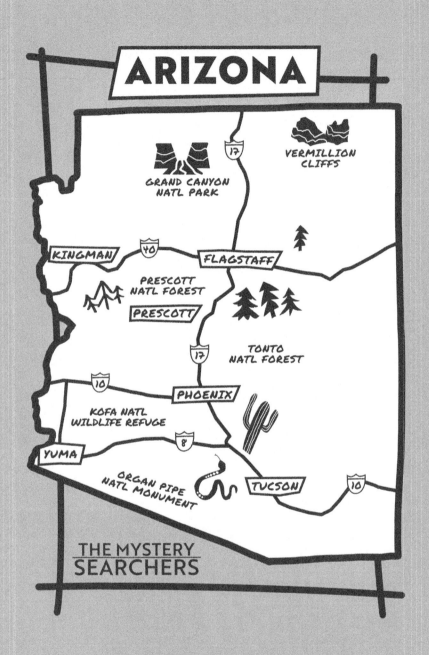

ARIZONA

VERMILLION CLIFFS

GRAND CANYON NATL PARK

17

KINGMAN

40

FLAGSTAFF

PRESCOTT NATL FOREST

PRESCOTT

TONTO NATL FOREST

17

10

PHOENIX

KOFA NATL WILDLIFE REFUGE

YUMA

8

ORGAN PIPE NATL MONUMENT

TUCSON

10

THE MYSTERY
SEARCHERS

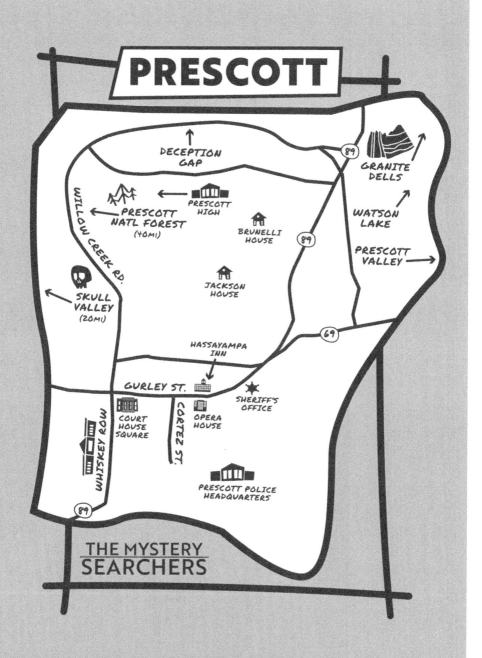

1

THE SWAMP

"*What is it?*" Kathy Brunelli yelled as she gazed up, shading her eyes from the blazing Arizona sun. "What do you see?"

Her brother, Pete, stood high on the adjacent bluff, right beside his buddy Tom. He cupped his hands and shouted back down to Kathy, his voice echoing off the surrounding cliffs. "*Wilderness!* . . . -*ness!* . . . -*ness!* . . ."

"Brilliant," Kathy groused to her best friend, Suzanne Jackson, Tom's twin sister. "Sometimes Pete can annoy me without even trying."

The two boys stepped back from the edge of the bluff and disappeared.

The treasure map showed water, close by too. But where? Suzanne glanced at the compass in her hand. "What are those guys *thinking*? If we follow the map, it's as obvious as the nose on your face—look where it ends." The girls eyed the document for the umpteenth time.

Kathy said, "Well, that big 'X' centers on water, that's for sure. Or at least, there was water when someone drew this map—but who knows how long ago *that* was."

The unknown "someone" had sketched the map in black ink

across the top half of an 8x11 folded sheet of writing paper. He—or she—had traced a journey from Prescott to Skull Valley, a twenty-mile jaunt through Arizona's spectacular high country. Then the trail jogged onto what had turned out to be a little-used gravel road, which split into two.

That's when things got interesting.

THE ADVENTURE HAD BEGUN TWO DAYS EARLIER WITH A TEXT MESSAGE from Mrs. Otto: *Hi, Suzie—Just received a raft of old books from an estate. See u soon.*

Mrs. Otto was the Jacksons' longtime friend and neighbor, and the manager of Prescott's St. Vincent de Paul Thrift Store. When it came to handling books, Mrs. Otto trusted Suzanne implicitly, and not just because Suzanne was such a book lover: she was also a confident young person, reliable and sure of herself, someone who knew where she was going in life. Yes, Mrs. Otto had seen Suzanne's famous temper flare, more than once too, but over the years she had watched as Suzanne slowly gained control of her fiery emotions.

The donation had appeared on the charity's loading dock at an unknown time during the night—dozens of tomes, all boxed up, in good condition or better. Old ones too. Ten boxes in total.

The anonymous gift bore a cryptic message, attached to one box with heavy packing tape: *The lady died.*

Suzanne hurried over on Monday morning. Her job—a part-time gig she loved—was to sort and price each book. An hour later, as she flipped through an early copy of *Wuthering Heights*, a folded sheet of paper slipped out and fluttered to the floor. Suzanne's heart skipped a beat—it wasn't the first time she had discovered treasure between the pages of a book.

There had been the forgotten tintype of a Confederate war officer. In perfect condition too—the thrift store sold it for seventy-five dollars. Once she had found an eighty-year-old birth certificate.

And, just last winter, a hundred-dollar bill had popped out of a famous historical novel. It looked pristine but dated back to the 1920s. *Wow.*

After that, Suzanne fanned every book. But finding a treasure map raised the ante to a whole new level.

"Oh, my goodness," Mrs. Otto said when Suzanne laid the find on her desk. Her eyes grew larger as she adjusted her glasses and tilted her head a touch. "I'm sure this is someone's idea of a joke. Still, you might check it out, dear. One never knows."

It was the title above the sketch—"My Treasure Map"—that fired up everyone's imagination. And beneath the drawing, written in cursive with a shaky hand, someone had penned a curious set of instructions:

> *Take Iron Springs Road (county road 10) to Skull Valley.*
> *Turn left on Copper Basin Road, 6.3 miles.*
> *Turn right to switch to the secondary road, go 1.3 miles. Park, and walk left along the dry creek road for half a mile.*
> *Watch for the water!*
> *Please help, whoever you are.*
> *Thank you.*

"Skull Valley? Treasure? *Man, oh, man,*" Pete had said when Suzanne showed the treasure map to the twins' best friends. He rubbed his hands together. Pete was the impetuous one who acted first, thought second, and often paid a price for his impulsiveness. "Can you *believe* it?"

TUESDAY MORNING FOUND THE FOURSOME WALKING ALONG AN OLD, wide track that ran parallel to a dry creek bed, twisting its way north. A century earlier, someone—miners, no doubt—had turned the route into a rough roadbed. But time had dredged up rocks and boulders, layering them against dead trees and broken, decaying branches, littering the track for as far as they could see. At one point, decades earlier, a gigantic desert saguaro had fallen along the route and rotted away to its skeletal remains.

The map's initial instructions—Iron Springs Road to Skull Valley, turn left on Copper Basin Road to a secondary road—had turned out, despite the passage of time, to have been easy enough to follow. But not even a 4x4 could have been able to negotiate the debris on the old miners' track, never mind the Brunellis' low-slung Mustang Hatchback.

Kathy parked at the side of the secondary road, and everyone prepared for the hike. But first the boys climbed that bluff, searching the arid land before them.

"Notice anything?" Tom asked.

"Nothing but an incredible view," Pete replied.

In the distance stretched the million-plus acres of Prescott National Forest, rising from low desert to mountain ranges over eight thousand feet high, and home to Grief Hill, Yellowjacket Gulch, Blind Indian Creek, and Horsethief Basin. Looking east, between where the boys stood on the rocky bluff and the western edge of the national wonder—lay an undulating and barren high-desert landscape: rock-strewn ravines, hidden canyons, sparse hills, cactus and trees.

"You can count on wild mule deer down there for sure," Tom said knowingly, "plus antelopes, cougars, bears." It was by no means their first desert hike.

"And snakes," Pete added with a wicked grin. "Western diamond-back rattlers. Kathy's favorite."

The boys raced down the far side of the bluff and crossed back over a canyon floor. Panting and out of breath, and despite being weighed down by their backpacks—with rope, an axe, a hammer, bear spray, flashlights, compasses and, most importantly, food—they soon caught up with the girls, who by this time were well ahead of them along the trail.

Tom admitted defeat. "Okay, you were right, Suzie. We couldn't spot a drop of water anywhere."

"*Told* you," she replied with a touch of exasperation. "The treasure map will find it for us. And we're close—according to the map, it's dead ahead. Let's keep going."

The desert floor felt frozen in time, utterly still without a hint of a breeze. The foursome's footsteps and labored breathing joined a million cicadas and the screeching alarms of overhead birds. A relentless sun beat down on them, intensifying as the minutes dragged by and midday approached, but they had dressed for it: shorts, cool tops, hiking boots, and hats.

Pete stopped for a giant swig of water. He removed his hat and ran fingers through his thick, black hair, soaked with perspiration. "Might be the only liquid out here," he cracked, holding up his canteen.

Suzanne rolled her eyes. "Get ready for a surprise." As the discoverer of the map, she felt the most invested in believing in its accuracy. In her mind, there wasn't a shred of doubt.

Soon, Kathy's pedometer clicked to point five. "We're close— watch yourselves."

The old mining track inclined a few degrees as it meandered between low canyon walls. Then it sloped up to a plateau with a gentle eastward turn before slipping downward into a ravine, and—

"*Water!*" Kathy cried.

They all raced forward. A good-sized, irregularly shaped pond stretched before them, looking as if it had swallowed the roadbed. The water's surface—coated with a slimy layer of decayed moss and other green matter—displayed tall, reed-like stalks that poked above it, stretching from murky depths into the fresh air above. A pungent smell of dead greenery assailed their nostrils.

"You call that water?" Tom said, more than astounded. "More like a *swamp*, I'd say."

"Boy, you're not kidding," Pete said. "So the old mining route heads straight into a slimy pool of—well, whatever this is. Then it climbs out of the ravine and continues north."

"Yeah, a hundred yards farther out," Suzanne said, sounding

more surprised than disappointed. She had anticipated water, not a stagnant desert oasis.

"No wonder we couldn't spot it from the bluff," Tom said, taking in the soaring canyon walls. "You realize how *deep* this ravine is?"

"It's deep all right," Kathy said. "We're in a natural bowl, surrounded on all four sides. The only open channel is this track, coming and going."

"Check out the chalky white deposits on the rock walls," Suzanne said. "Calcium, I bet. The water has receded since spring."

"So the treasure's . . . here?" Kathy said. She held the map in both hands in front of her.

"It sure looks that way," Pete replied, peering over her shoulder and jabbing the X. "And that's where we are. Whoever drew this map knew the area well."

Kathy knelt and slipped a finger into the water, pushing aside a thin layer of slime. "I'll tell you what," she said. "No way am I jumping into *that* to look for anything."

"You big baby," Pete teased with a grin. "Me, I'll go in there. But first I need food to fortify me."

"I'm with you, buddy," Tom said, clapping his best friend on the back. "Eating, I mean." Laughter rang out.

Soon, a blanket lay stretched over a flat slab of rock beside the murky pond. Each one of the hungry four found a spot to relax. They unpacked sandwiches and snacks and passed around bottles of water.

"I wonder what's hiding in there," Suzanne wondered aloud.

"You don't think there are snakes under the slime, do you?" Kathy asked in all seriousness. She wrinkled her nose.

A thought popped into Tom's head. "No clue, but you can bet this must be the watering hole for the local wildlife."

"That's why I packed bear spray," Pete said. "You can't ever know what you'll encounter out in the wilderness. Not only that, but it's possible the treasure's in a nearby cave."

That threw his sister into a conniption of laughter. "Oh, yeah. And that imaginary cave might hide a fat, hungry black bear, right?"

"Wouldn't be the first time."

"We'll follow you in," Kathy added.

"Kind of you, I'm sure."

"Whoa, that never crossed my mind," Suzanne interrupted, looping back to her brother's comment. She cast her nervous eyes around the ravine, searching for signs of wildlife. "Slime or no slime, this is the only water for miles. We need to head out long before sunset."

"Yeah," Pete said grinning, "before that bear gets thirsty."

His sister gave him a good poke in the side.

Their discussion next centered on how to explore the pond. Tom suggested building a raft and measuring the depth with a sheared-off tree branch.

"No way," Suzanne countered. "Too time consuming."

Pete liked the branch idea. "We can plunge it in there and see what we're dealing with. Any sandwiches left?"

Minutes later, as Kathy peered across the swamp, she caught a glint in the afternoon sun. *What is that?* she wondered. Without saying a word, she stood and walked to where the miner's track vanished beneath the water. She paced along the water's edge, varying her angle of vision, before dropping to one knee.

Suzanne munched on an apple. "What's up, Kathy?" she called out between bites. "What are you looking at?"

"Oh, I'm just checking out this vehicle sunk in the swamp," she replied innocently, eyeing her brother.

"Vehicle!" the other three chorused.

Pete stood up. "What on earth are you talking about?"

Kathy giggled and pointed ahead, toward the pond's dead center. She loved one-upping her brother. "Check it out. What's sticking out of the water, a foot high, between all those stalks?"

The three hurried over. Silence descended as they peered across the murky surface, following Kathy's pointing finger. A thin sliver of metal protruded above the layer of slime, almost hidden by a forest of reeds. It had a tiny nodule on top, and its peeling chrome was pocked with rusty brown patches. Not twenty yards from where they stood.

Tom broke the silence. "It's an antenna!"

"Oh, sure, I see it," Suzanne said. "The old-fashioned kind."

"Like the one on our Mustang," Pete said.

"Uh-huh, no kidding," Kathy said, poking her brother once more. "And I'd bet anything the treasure is inside this one."

2

A DISCOVERY

A treasure hunt had spun into something quite unexpected. From the bottom of the murky pond, a mystery had emerged.

And there was *nothing* the foursome liked better.

In fact, the Jackson/Brunelli team had earned quite a reputation for mystery solving. *The Daily Pilot*—Prescott, Arizona's hometown newspaper—had covered the exploits of "the mystery searchers," as it had dubbed them. More than once too. The nickname had stuck.

Perhaps the person most responsible for this was the twins' father, Edward Jackson—*Chief* Edward Jackson of the Prescott City Police. Dinnertime conversation at the Jacksons' often focused on a "whodunit," some drama of crime and mystery that played out across the kitchen table. Inevitably, there were many questions and precious few answers—police matters were highly confidential. That only made things all the more intriguing.

Aware that his twins wished to follow him into law enforcement, and proud of their interest, the Chief encouraged it. In fact, his support had included putting the resources of Prescott City Police at their disposal from time to time.

The twins' mother, Sherri—a well-liked at-home social worker for Yavapai County—didn't share their enthusiasm. Far from it, actually. Her two favorite words, the twins often said, were *dangerous* and *caution*. A third one she bandied about was *risky*. But they loved their mother dearly.

Mystery solving had rubbed off on the Jackson twins' best friends, Pete and Kathy Brunelli, too. The four Prescott kids had grown up together. Bosom buddies at St. Francis Elementary School, they had remained close as they graduated into Prescott High.

Now, standing at the edge of the murky pond during summer break, the tall, willowy, fair-haired twins and their two friends of Italian heritage—shorter, both with coal-dark hair and olive-hued skin—glanced at one another in astonishment.

Suzanne asked, "How on earth—"

"Did a car end up in there?" Kathy finished for her. "And on this track too. It's impassible by car!"

"And when?" Pete wondered.

"Good questions," Tom said. "Let's jump in and see what's up."

"Great," Pete said, brimming with excitement. He loved adventure. "We'll need a large tree branch. We can use it to push the slime aside." He raced over to his backpack and retrieved an ax.

The four of them spread out, searching for something to use as a float. A minute later, Suzanne shouted, "Got it!" She brandished an old, dried-out cottonwood limb, six feet long, lying beside the creek bed.

"Perfect," Tom said. "We'll use it as our slime pushing floater."

Pete chopped away a few lifeless branches before they hauled the dead bough over to the water's edge and plopped it in. The boys removed their hiking boots and socks.

"No way am I taking off *my* boots," Suzanne objected. "Who knows what's at the bottom of this swamp?"

Kathy pulled a face and glanced at her best friend. "You're not going *in* there?" The very idea made her squeamish.

"Wouldn't miss it for the world," Suzanne replied, flashing a grin.

Soon enough, they slid the dead limb into the pond, splashing around for a few moments to drive away the slime. Then the four shoved off—Kathy plugged her nose—all hanging onto the limb, walking, kicking, and floating toward the antenna as the water grew deeper. Their footsteps stirred up a fearsome cloud of mud, staining the murky blue-green color a turgid brown.

"I hit something," Pete said, his voice rising a decimal or two. "Gotta be the vehicle." He climbed up what felt like two steps or levels of something until he was standing with the water only up to his shins.

Suzanne was right behind him. "We're standing on the roof, I think." She thrust an arm into the pond, touching the roof's rounded edge, rough with age. "This thing is pointing due north."

"It sure is," Tom said, feeling with his bare feet.

"I'll bet it's rusted right out," Pete said. "Car or truck, whataya think?"

Suzanne said, "Who knows? Could be a van."

Kathy touched the antenna before joining the other three on the roof. "I figure this water is about six feet deep."

Splash! Pete dived in and disappeared for thirty seconds. He surfaced, hideous green slime hanging over his forehead and across his nose, gulping for air. "It's a car. Don't step on the bottom if you can avoid it—it's real mucky down there. There's a foot-deep layer of goo that swirls up and blinds you."

"*E-e-w,*" Kathy cried, screwing up her face.

The twins slipped back into the water. Pete followed, but his sister refused.

Half a minute later, the three searchers popped up. "Yeah, a car for sure," Suzanne said. "Try it, Kathy. The water's nice and cool down there."

"I touched the windshield," Pete said. "Too dark to see anything."

"Kathy," Tom said, "swim back and get the flashlight. Put it in one of those ziplock sandwich bags and seal it."

"Okay," she replied. She forced herself to dive in. The slime had more or less floated away, and the water had returned to a hazy

11

blue-green—the invading brown had dissipated. She soon returned, holding a flashlight with one arm above her head.

Tom held out his hand and pulled Kathy onto the car's trunk. He clicked the flashlight on through the plastic bag. "Okay, Pete, let's go."

The boys dived in. Clouds of algae raced by, caught by the cone of light as it dimly revealed the vehicle resting in six feet of water. Its flat tires, shredded by rot, had sunk into a deep layer of muck. They had arrived on the passenger's side, close to the front, and held themselves down by clinging to the bottom edge of the chassis. The hood was punctuated by what looked like twin air-intake vents, almost like machine nostrils, side by side in the middle, close to the windshield, and a rusted symbol: 383. With little remaining air, they shot to the surface.

Between gasps, Pete said, "Whoa, that car is in *rough* shape."

"You would be too," his sister said, "if you were under water for a few decades."

Pete, an aspiring engineer, was a car buff. He had studied classic automobiles for years and relished the one he and his sister drove— their historic Mustang Hatchback. "It's an old Dodge muscle car, famous too. You know what this means?"

"Sure," Suzanne said. "It means the old wreck has rusted away in this watery grave for decades." She held one hand out. "Now it's our turn."

Pete grimaced as Tom passed the flashlight to his sister.

"Come on, Kathy! This is fun."

The two girls dived in and angled to the front of the vehicle, grasping onto to the front bumper. Kathy played the flashlight's beam over the rusted orange-red-brown wreck, the image appearing to undulate like a mirage.

An Arizona license plate emerged from the darkness, warped and partially rusted through but still legible: B3546. Kathy thought the plate dated to 1970, but rust had eaten away the top half of the last number. *Maybe 1978?* she wondered. Farther up, above a front grill caved in at the center, the vehicle's brand name materialized in what must once have been shiny chrome letters: DODGE. And above that rested a small, rusted insignia in the shape of a bee. Kathy ran a finger over it before they popped to the surface.

"B3546," Suzanne shouted, gasping for air. "That's the license plate number. B3546."

Kathy took deep breaths. "I think the plate says 1970. It's a Dodge with a strange insignia, like a bee floating above the name."

"It's a Dodge Super Bee!" Pete exclaimed. "Wow." He ripped the flashlight out of Suzanne's hand and jumped into the water. "Our turn."

Kathy shot her brother a withering look. "You know, you could ask first."

The boys descended to the rear of the vehicle, where Pete fanned the flashlight beam across a DODGE logo centered between two long, ribbed taillights. Back in the seventies, he knew, dual license plates had been standard, and *1970* appeared clearly on the rear plate. The boys pulled themselves along the driver's side, past the left rear quarter panel, before their air ran low. Then they bubbled to the surface.

"One more time!" Tom shouted. "Let's check the side windows." They descended again, this time latching onto the driver's-side door handle of the two-door hardtop. Pete was surprised to find the window open three-quarters of the way. He reached the flashlight inside cautiously, gliding it back and forth, aiming the beam toward the dashboard. A ghostly steering wheel emerged in the grainy haze, and behind it the dash, its speedometer forever stopped at zero. But both boys' eyes locked onto on a weird whiteness reflecting through the algae-filled water on the passenger side. Pete tapped Tom before they kicked up again.

"You see that?" Tom asked, floating as he pushed his hair back from his eyes. "That white thing?"

"Yeah, what the heck was it?"

"Gimme," Kathy demanded, holding out her hand. "We'll check it out."

Suzanne said, "Fair is fair."

The boys glanced at each other before reluctantly handing over the flashlight.

"Go to the passenger side." Tom said.

The girls slipped down together, dropping to the vehicle's right side. They grasped the door handle, using the car itself for ballast. Kathy slid the flashlight back and forth against the passenger door glass—unlike the driver's window, it was closed tight—angling the beam of light up and down, right to left. The boys were right—there was *something* white in the murky blue-green darkness inside.

The girls pressed their noses to the glass. A long moment passed before, all at once, looking down from that angle, a shocking realization dawned on them at the same time.

A disconnected skull—somehow wedged between the window and bench passenger seat—stared at the two girls from its sightless, hollow eye sockets, an inch away. Below it lay the remains of a human skeleton. slumped and twisted across the front passenger bench seat.

3

A MISSING HEIR

"Oh, I can't *believe* it!" Suzanne cried, gulping for air. "Give me a hand up."

Tom reached down and pulled his sister to the roof. *"What? What'd you see?"*

Kathy surfaced at the same time. "Gives a new meaning to the name Skull Valley."

"What are you talking about?" Pete asked.

"There's a skeleton in that car," Suzanne replied, trying in vain to push the image out of her mind.

"A skeleton?"

"Yes!" Kathy said. "Staring at us, and this close too." She held out her thumb and forefinger stretched an inch apart, her eyes blazing. "Freaked me right out and just think—we've been swimming around in that . . . that—"

"Stuff," Pete finished for her. A strange expression crossed his face—halfway between euphoria and repulsion. He glanced at Tom. *"Let's go!"* He grabbed the flashlight, and the boys dived off the roof. Thirty seconds later they were back.

"Okay," Pete said. "No doubt about what that is."

"Right? This is a crime scene," Tom said. "Let's get out of here."

"A crime scene," Kathy repeated in surprise. "How do you know that? It might have been an accident."

"When the cause of death is a mystery, the police open a criminal investigation," Suzanne explained. You learn certain things when your father is the chief of police. "But it sure looks like a drowning —accidental, or otherwise."

"Well, no matter what, it's a mystery," Tom said.

"That's for sure," Pete said. "We've got the 'when' and 'where' down. Now it's time for the 'who', 'what', and 'why'."

"'Where' was the easy part," Kathy said. "Only took fifty years, give or take."

PRESCOTT, ARIZONA IS ONE OF THOSE SLEEPY LITTLE CITIES WHERE nothing much ever seems to happen. Unless, of course, your father happens to be the chief of police. Then it's a whole different ballgame.

The twins patiently waited for their parents to return from a late-night dinner. They *had* to talk with their father—he was always the first person they turned to for advice about a new case. It was after ten o'clock when a car pulled into the garage. Tom had the coffeepot on the burner.

"We've got a new mystery," Suzanne said, her brown eyes dancing as she greeted her parents with hugs. She set four empty cups on the kitchen table. "You won't believe this one."

"Try me," the Chief said, grinning.

"I hope it's not dangerous," their mother said, pulling out a chair.

"No, not at all," Tom assured her. "But intriguing, for sure."

A day earlier, their parents had viewed the treasure map when Suzanne returned from the thrift store, excited to show her latest "find." Now, the twins filled them in on the day's hunt.

Tom got to the part where they discovered that the sunken vehicle was a Dodge Super Bee.

The Chief set his coffee down on the kitchen table and perked right up. "A Dodge Super Bee," he repeated. His eyes bored into Tom. "You sure about that?"

"Very. And it had 1970 license plates, front and back."

"Did you get the plate number?"

"B3546."

"Arizona plates?" the Chief asked.

"Yes."

Suzanne picked up the story. "After Kathy and I dived in for the third time, we swam to the passenger side of the car and shone the flashlight in to scan the interior. Guess what was inside?" Her voice quivered.

"The treasure?" Sherri replied, wide-eyed.

"Nope. A skeleton," Tom answered.

"*A skeleton!*" Sherri cried. A look of horror crossed her face. "Oh, my Lord. You must have flipped out!"

"*Freaked* out," Suzanne said. "The skull was just an inch from my nose."

Her mother's eyebrows rose.

"No, Mom, we're serious, aren't we, Tom?" Suzanne pushed a lock of amber hair from her eyes as she looked to her brother for support. "I thought Kathy would pass out. The thing had turned our way. Like it was staring at us."

Tom said, "Yup, no doubt at all. Pete and I saw it too."

They could see the Chief's mind churning. "No evidence of a body on the driver's side?"

"None," Tom replied.

The Chief stood and retrieved pen and paper from his briefcase. Then he reached for his cell phone and placed a call. He stepped out of the kitchen, returning a minute later.

"Where's the treasure map?"

"Upstairs," Suzanne replied. She stood and raced to the stairs.

"Two-door or four-door?" he asked Tom.

"Two-door."

"Hardtop or sedan?"

"Hardtop."

17

"How deep?"

"The water? We figured six feet where the car is resting, but the pond slopes down. It's possible it could hit ten feet at the deep end."

Suzanne hurried back. She unfolded the treasure map and carefully laid it in front of her parents.

The Chief stared at the document with practiced eyes. He rubbed a corner of the page between two fingers. "What strikes you about this document?" he asked. "I don't mean the map or the words themselves."

"The handwriting looks like Grandma's," Suzanne offered.

"Good observation," said the Chief. "Old-fashioned cursive handwriting, plus a trembling hand. *Probably* an older person. Anything else?"

"An older person, but not old paper," Tom said. "The car's license plates say 1970, but this paper feels new."

"Right," said the Chief. He paused for a moment. "You mentioned the driver's window was down partway. What about the passenger's window?"

"Shut tight," Suzanne replied.

"Half a mile off the gravel road?"

"Just over."

The Chief's cell phone buzzed. "Chief Jackson here." A long pause ensued. "Okay, I figured as much . . . No, not a word to anyone, otherwise we'll have everyone and his dog out there . . . Yeah, I'll call the sheriff tomorrow morning . . . Sure, thanks." He disconnected.

"What is it?" Sherri asked.

The Chief reached over for the coffee pot. "Anyone else for more?"

"I'll have some, Dad," Tom said. His father poured.

"Well," the Chief said, eyeing the twins, "it's my belief that you found the most famous missing person in Prescott's history."

"You've *got* to be kidding!" Sherri exclaimed

"Who was missing, Dad? Who was it?" Tom asked, his heart pounding.

Suzanne was beside herself. "And how do you know?"

The Chief glanced away to compose his thoughts. "Well, it was long before my time. But you mentioned a Dodge Super Bee with 1970 license plates. You don't forget a car like that. Trust me, when that car and the individual driving it disappeared, this city turned upside down."

His words triggered a distant memory for Sherri. "Oh, sure, that's right. I remember hearing something about that when I was little."

"Yeah," the Chief continued, "it was the never-ending story. The person who owned that make and model vanished without a trace. In fact, that cold case is still on our books all these years later. The press went crazy, and the pressure on the various local police departments—well, *intense* is an understatement." He paused.

"Even the FBI got involved," their father added. "The authorities assumed kidnapping—he came from a wealthy family—but as the months rolled by, no one demanded a ransom for the boy. The whole state was looking for a fire-engine-red Super Bee."

He stopped, glancing over at the twins. "Half a century passed before you found it."

"Kathy and Pete too," Suzanne said.

"There wasn't a fleck of paint left on that car," Tom said, picturing the rusty-orange chassis sunk in murky water.

"Sure, no surprise—rust has eaten the paint away," the Chief said. "But how many 1970 Dodge Super Bees are under six feet of water . . . in Arizona?"

Seconds ticked by.

"Well, *who was it?*" Sherri asked, visibly annoyed. She raised a hand, palm up. "You're keeping us all in suspense."

"His name was Grant Dorrance Hutchinson," her husband replied calmly. "He was seventeen years old when he vanished without a trace. The young man came from the richest family in Prescott. His grandfather made a fortune in silver mining, and his father was a city alderman."

"Silver mining," Tom repeated. "There's a good chance he was familiar with the old roadbed."

"Maybe," Suzanne said, somewhat puzzled. "How come Grandad forgot to tell him about the pond?"

The Chief paused for a few moments and sipped his coffee. "So when you mentioned the car—and 1970—well, it was obvious. That license plate confirmed it."

"What a tragedy," Sherri said. As a seasoned Yavapai County social worker, she had years of experience dealing with bereaved families. "This will be bittersweet for the survivors."

"If there are any," the Chief said. "I would imagine his parents have passed. There was a sibling—a sister, as I recall. We'll dig for answers tomorrow." He stifled a yawn. "But I'll tell you something. This is a big story. The media will cover it like nothing we've ever seen in this town."

"You'll treat the pond as a crime scene, right?" Tom asked.

"Oh, for sure," the Chief replied. "But not for Prescott City Police —Skull Valley is outside my jurisdiction. Sheriff Steve McClennan will take over tomorrow morning."

The twins glanced at each other with knowing looks. *No problem.* The sheriff of Yavapai County was an old family friend who had assisted them on previous mysteries.

"And this won't be an ordinary crime scene," The Chief said. "He'll open a manslaughter or murder investigation."

"So if it's *not* an accident," Suzanne said, locking eyes with her father, "then you suspect . . ."

"I didn't say that," the Chief corrected his daughter.

Tom thought out loud, a trait he had inherited from his father. "Hutchinson's skeleton ended up on the passenger side, probably carried by the water. But if someone else was in the car at the time of the accident—"

"If it *was* an accident," Suzanne said, picking up her brother's thread. "That person *must* have escaped out the driver's side open window."

"Leaving Hutchinson to drown!" Tom finished triumphantly.

"Anything's possible," their father said. His right index finger shot up. "But we're getting ahead of ourselves. First, *if* someone was in the vehicle with Mr. Hutchinson when the car sank, then yes: he or she would have escaped through the open window. That individual would then have *deserted* the young man without notifying authorities. That would be a serious charge. It could even be manslaughter."

"But it *could* also be murder," Tom said. "What if Grant Hutchinson was already dead before the car went into the water?"

"Right!" Suzanne said. "And someone just pushed the car into the pond? Or, what if Grant wasn't dead, but just unconscious?"

"The big question," Tom said, "is, who was the unknown person who escaped? Wouldn't it be the same individual who penned the treasure map?"

The Chief stood and stretched. It had turned into a late night, and the next morning promised to be a busy one. "Too early to tell," the Chief said. "And murder could be a stretch. Still, that skeleton might tell us a thing or two."

"Whoever drew the treasure map escaped from the submerged Dodge," Tom said in a firm voice. "Who else would know the way out there?"

"That makes perfect sense," Suzanne said. "And then they felt guilty after."

"Guilty?" the Chief asked. An amused look crossed his face.

"You bet." Suzanne said. "How does the note end?" She read aloud: "'Please help, whoever you are . . . Thank you.'"

"A guilty cry for help," Sherri said, agreeing with her daughter.

"My hunch is it was a woman—and that she was getting ready to meet her maker," Suzanne said. "You agreed, Dad, that you could tell by the shaky handwriting that it was an elderly person."

"Now I understand the title, 'My Treasure Map,'" Tom said. "Her treasure—if it really was a woman who wrote the note—was Grant Dorrance Hutchinson."

"For sure," Suzanne stated emphatically. "Alive *or* dead!" She shook her long ponytail in wonder.

"That's a lot of conjecture," the Chief said. He yawned again. "It's time for bed."

"One other thing I should have mentioned," Suzanne said. "When those books came into the store, we found a note taped to one box. It read, 'The lady died.'"

"Okay, sure," the Chief said. "That could make sense. Then before she passed on, the woman created this treasure map. She wanted the world to know." He rinsed his empty cup and set it down in the dish drainer. "Here's another thing. I'll bet the book hiding the map was a valuable one. Am I right?"

"Oh, yes," Suzanne replied. "It was an early edition of *Wuthering Heights*. The thrift store will sell it for three hundred dollars. How did you figure that out?"

"She wanted a thoughtful person to discover the map. A serious reader who loves classic books, a person confident, interested, and full of life . . . an individual who would act upon a treasure map that appeared to be real, and not throw it away or hide it in a drawer and forget about it."

He leaned over and touched his daughter's nose. "Someone just like you, Suzie."

4

A HIKE BACK

"Way too early," Suzanne complained with a yawn. She padded into the kitchen and grabbed a box of cornflakes.

"Don't use all the milk," her brother admonished.

She glanced over at his hair, the identical auburn color of hers, sticking up in every direction. "You forgot to comb your hair this morning."

It was six o'clock, Wednesday morning. First up was a phone call to Sheriff McClennan. The twins—still in their pajamas—were pumped. *Who wouldn't be?* They sat down with their father at the breakfast table as he touched the number in his mobile phone's address book. Sherri poured coffee for everyone.

"Sorry to wake you so early, Sheriff. I think I may have a bit of a surprise for you. Do you recall the case of Grant Dorrance Hutchinson? . . . Yup, that's him, all right. Vanished without a trace. Well, our four homegrown mystery searchers located his 1970 Dodge Super Bee . . . Un-huh, the license plates check out . . . it's submerged in a desert pond near Skull Valley . . . Yes, lots of water . . . No, not a doubt . . . And there's a skeleton in the car that I'm assuming are the remains of the missing young man . . . Yeah, they're with me now. I'll put you on speaker."

The sheriff's voice was rock steady—nothing ever seemed to faze him. "So where exactly has Grant Dorrance Hutchinson been hiding all these years?"

"Eight miles east of Skull Valley off Copper Basin Road," Suzanne replied. "In six feet of slimy water."

"Full of algae," Tom added. "Very mucky bottom too, that gets stirred up if you step in it. Hard to see underwater, and it's stagnant too."

"Not surprising nobody ever found him," the sheriff said. "That's the middle of nowhere. I'm surprised there's water out there. How far off the road?"

"Just over half a mile," Tom replied.

"Can you drive in?"

"Well, it's an old miner's route covered with rocks and dead trees."

"Okay, I've got a wrecker that will negotiate the debris. Care to meet me out there?"

"Sure. When?"

"How about ten o'clock this morning? In Skull Valley beside the post office? I'll need you to show us the way."

"We'll be there," Tom promised.

"It's amazing you even found him," the sheriff said. "Good for you."

"Enough water had evaporated that the car's aerial was sticking out of the surface," Suzanne said.

"Yes, indeed, a lucky break," the sheriff said. "This case has dragged on for decades. I hope you're ready—it's a big deal. National media will be all over this."

"We'll handle them," the Chief said with a grim countenance. He wasn't a fan of the out-of-town press, who were often pushy and even just plain rude. The local media, especially Heidi Hoover, the star reporter of Prescott's hometown newspaper, *The Daily Pilot*, had a much more cooperative relationship with the local police.

"I wonder if the reward is still active," the sheriff said, almost to himself.

The twins glanced at each other. "Reward?"

"Yeah. The family offered a hundred grand for Grant Hutchinson's release, or fifty grand for his body. Back then, they assumed kidnapping. But no one ever demanded a ransom or claimed the reward."

"Dad told us," Suzanne said.

"Well," the Chief said, "no clue about the reward, but I'd guess we can rule out kidnapping. I believe there are no survivors—with the possible exception of one sibling. And I'm not even sure *she's* alive."

Moments later, the twins called the Brunellis and dragged them out of bed. A ten-minute phone call ensured, bringing their friends up to date.

"Can you *believe* it?" Pete exclaimed. "There *was* treasure out there."

"What are you talking about?" his sister asked.

"The reward, silly! Maybe it's still active."

Kathy ignored him. "Just think. Prescott's most famous missing-persons case, and I found his car. Wow."

"You did *not*," Pete said, censuring his sister. "*We* did. Can all of us head out to Skull Valley?" he asked the twins.

Suzanne laughed. "You bet. Let's go together."

"We'll pick you up at nine thirty," Pete offered.

Kathy asked, "What about Heidi? Shouldn't we clue her in?"

"Oh, for sure," Tom said. "She needs to get the story first."

Heidi Hoover was not only *The Daily Pilot*'s top reporter—she was also their good friend. She had assisted them with other cases, once even sharing in some reward money. And in the case that Heidi had dubbed the Secret of the Mysterious Mansion, Heidi's fast-thinking actions had led to their rescue.

Suzanne messaged her. *Heidi—We have found the missing 1970 Dodge Super Bee belonging to Grant Dorrance Hutchinson. Please call.*

"Watch," Tom said, chuckling out loud. "I'll give her sixty seconds."

Sure enough, Suzanne's phone buzzed, close to the minute mark.

"Who the heck is he?" Heidi asked. "I've never heard of the guy. Nineteen-seventy is a long time ago." The twins filled her in.

"Whoa!" she exclaimed. "There'll be a media storm, you can count on it. A skeleton—and the richest family in Prescott, missing for half a century. You guys are up to your armpits in another mystery."

"Not many people know," Suzanne said. "Sheriff McClennan will yank the car out of the water this morning. Meet us at the Skull Valley post office at ten."

"Okay," Heidi said. It was easy to tell she was cranked up. "I'll bring a photographer with me. In the meantime, I'll ransack the archives. See you soon—and thanks for the lead!" She disconnected.

THE FOUR MYSTERY SEARCHERS PULLED UP TO THE SKULL VALLEY post office, right on time, shocked to find a contingent of vehicles in the parking lot. They joined a group of people surrounding a huge wrecker tow truck that doubled as a flatbed. Sheriff McClennan and the Chief were leaning against the truck, talking.

"Good morning," the sheriff said. He shook hands with each of them. "Nice to work with you again." He winked. "And a splendid job, I might add. Let me introduce you to a few of my friends."

They met the medical examiner for Yavapai County, Dr. Brent Walker, a tall, thin guy with a serious demeanor, plus a diver from the Sheriff's Office, Officer Meg O'Brien. There were two other deputies present and the wrecker's driver, Hank. After Hank had pulled the Dodge to dry land, crime scene technicians would sift for evidence. Still and video photographers would document events as they unfolded. Together, they had loaded a ton of equipment onto the back of the wrecker.

The number of people surprised Kathy. "Thirteen of us altogether—it's a party!" she joked. Her brother could barely contain his excitement.

"Make that fifteen," Tom said. Heidi and her photographer had just pulled into a parking space. Heidi jumped out of her car first and hurried over, her tight black curls bouncing everywhere.

"Okay, let's roll," the sheriff said.

Heidi filled the foursome in on her research. "Not much to report. The kid and his car disappeared from the face of the earth August 1, 1970. Never seen again. It was a huge deal because the family was super wealthy and well known. The police figured it was a kidnapping that went bad. But no ransom was every demanded. Everyone assumed after a time that Grant must be dead. End of story—until now."

"What about his parents?" Kathy wondered aloud.

"Dead."

"Any siblings still alive?" Suzanne asked.

"One sister, two years younger. I couldn't find a thing on her. She seems to have disappeared, like her brother, except that no one noticed. Interestingly, there are reports of attempted kidnappings— of *her*—a year or so after Grant's disappearance."

"*Kidnappings?*" Tom asked. "You mean like . . . more than one?"

"Two."

Pete reacted in surprise. "How often does that happen?"

The noisy wrecker had monster tires that rolled over and around rocks and dead trees as if they didn't exist. Everyone else— they were all dressed for a hike, even the Chief wore jeans—fell in behind the truck.

Suzanne and Kathy walked beside the friendly diver. "Call me Meg," she told them.

"So you're a full-time officer *and* a diver?"

"Yes," the young woman said, smiling. "I'm a patrol officer, but I was a scuba diver as a kid, so whenever something like this comes up, they bring me in. How did you guys find the skeleton?"

The two girls related the story.

"No kidding," Meg said, "a treasure map. Good for you." Suzanne shared the twins' dream of following their father's footsteps into law enforcement.

"Oh, your dad is Chief Jackson? I've met him once before—he

and the sheriff are close friends. Well, you'll enjoy your future occupation. It's seldom boring, as you can see."

Meanwhile, the boys hiked in together beside the medical examiner as Heidi listened closely.

Tom had a question. "Dr. Walker, that skeleton has been in the pond for half a century. What can it tell you?"

"Oh, it'll have a story, for sure. Its teeth and bones should give us a good approximation of age. For example, if the permanent teeth are in, he or she reached late childhood. Or if there are wisdom teeth, the person was past eighteen years. Also, there are markers that will tell us the person's sex."

"What about height and weight?" Pete asked.

"Sure," the doctor replied. "The femur is one quarter of the body's entire length, so we can approximate the individual's height. Weight is more of a guess based on bone structure."

Tom asked, "Any intact DNA after all this time in the water?"

"There's a good chance," the doctor replied. "In a pond out here, I would expect low concentrations of salts, and relatively high levels of minerals like calcium and magnesium. Those factors improve DNA integrity."

The medical examiner stopped for a moment and scanned their faces. "Not only that, but broken bones or other evidence of blunt-force trauma or blade injuries could suggest foul play."

"'Foul play,'" Heidi repeated. Surprise had crept into her voice. "That thought never crossed my mind. I had assumed this was an accidental drowning."

"Oh sure, that's possible too," Dr. Clark replied. "But I've seen enough of these to know: a case can turn on a dime—straight into murder."

5

A SKELETON TALKS

Twenty minutes later, the wrecker plateaued and turned east before coming to a jarring halt. Below it was the desert ravine, with its gigantic basin of stagnant water sheltering a submerged Dodge Super Bee.

And one as-yet-unidentified skeleton.

"We're here!" Pete shouted.

The wrecker's reverse lights flickered on as its backup alert rang out. Everyone walked past the huge truck and down to the pond. The noise was so loud that Kathy plugged her ears.

"It stinks to high heaven," Suzanne complained about the diesel-powered monster.

"Smells worse than the swamp," Kathy quipped.

The wrecker negotiated a slow, torturous turnaround. Ten minutes passed before it edged up to the water's edge and lurched to a clanking halt. Hank jumped out of the cabin.

The equipment hit the ground with soft thuds. Officer O'Brien—Meg—donned her diving suit and an oxygen tank.

"So it's down six feet?" she confirmed with the girls.

"Uh-huh, about twenty yards from where we're standing," Kathy replied, pointing across the pond. "Can you see the antenna?"

It took a few moments to register. "Sure do. What direction is the car facing?"

"Due north."

Meg slipped into the water for a survey, pushing the slime before her. Once again, a muddy brown cloud bloomed in the blue-green color before she disappeared beneath the surface. The video camera Meg wore above her diving mask clicked on while the photographer captured still images from the shore. Three minutes later, she emerged, ready to attach the metal tow hook. She dragged it into the pond and vanished once more.

But not for long. Meg emerged, shouting, "Okay, Hank! It's all yours."

He shot her a thumbs-up and jumped into the wrecker's cabin. The huge chain extending from the rear of the truck emitted a tremendous cranking sound and went taut. The engine ramped higher, and a grinding noise started. A minute passed before the Dodge began its emergence from the watery grave, its first foray into fresh air and sunshine in decades. The bumper and rear license plate surfaced at a crawl . . . then the trunk . . . the back window . . . the roof, a rusted-orange color like the rest of the vehicle . . . and then the entire car, water sloshing away, winched onto dry land.

Free at last. Half a century after it had sunk—or *been sunk*.

The monster truck's engine slipped into neutral as the clanking of the chain stopped. Silence descended as technicians stepped over to the hulk. Two men worked on the driver's side door, trying to force it. It opened with a gush of cloudy brown liquid that whooshed out onto the ground.

On the passenger's side, the dropping water level revealed the skull, still locked between the bench seat and window, staring out with its unseeing eyes. Kathy shuddered.

Dr. Walker stepped over and dropped a thin, hard-plastic stretcher onto a rocky slab. He covered it with a wide, black plastic sheet. Meanwhile, police technicians explored inside the car, front and back, leaving space for the medical examiner to do his work. Then they pried the trunk open with a metal bar.

The crowd watched at a distance, quiet and respectful. Every so often a soft murmur arose. At one point, the Chief walked over to the four young mystery searchers.

"Your first experience with a dead body," he said in a low voice, searching their faces. "I can tell you: no one ever gets used to this."

"It's actually our second time," Kathy said. "We introduced ourselves yesterday."

Not much later, the sheriff ambled over. "My techs say the key's still in the ignition in the on-position. Same for the headlights knob—it's pulled on. There's little in that car except the remains of a wallet and a clutch purse. Everything in the purse disintegrated, and the wallet's in rough shape too. What looks like an Arizona driver's license shows the first two letters of a name—G and r... Grant, I assume. Nothing else in there but the skeleton."

"So he *is* the treasure," Suzanne reasoned out loud.

"You could be right," the sheriff said.

"I have a question," Pete asked. "How did that car get out here? I mean, rocks and debris cover the roadbed—it's darn near impassible."

"Well," Sheriff McClennan replied, "the track didn't always look this way. All these old mining routes were open until the hundred-year flood in 1978, long before your time. That event dragged in the mess you see here."

"You mean," Tom asked, "before 1978 this track was clear?"

"Yes, for sure. In 1970, that Dodge Super Bee would have cruised unimpeded and right into the pond. And at a good speed too."

"How did the miners build the track?" Pete asked. "They'd never get past this flooded basin."

"Oh, I'm sure the water dries up, if only every few decades," the sheriff replied. "That happens in the high desert."

Half an hour later, Dr. Walker had finished laying the skeleton on the plastic-lined stretcher, assembling it piece by piece like a giant jigsaw puzzle—*An awful one*, Suzanne thought, backing away at the sight. Tom, always the least squeamish of the four, looked on, fascinated. Technicians then folded over the plastic sheet and zippered it up—it was, Pete observed, like a specialized cross between a body bag and an evidence bag. Deputies lifted the stretcher and carried it over to the wrecker, pushing it along to the front of the flatbed.

"Go ahead," the sheriff said to Hank, spinning his hand in the air. "Pull the car up."

The clanking noise began again as the wrecker's engine ramped to a higher level. Five minutes later, the rescued vehicle sat behind the skeleton, riding high on the truck bed, ready for its final trip to the impound lot. There, crime technicians would pore over it, inch by inch.

With the roaring sound of its engine and great billows of smelly diesel exhaust, the wrecker headed back toward Skull Valley. A profound silence descended upon the scene as Dr. Walker walked over to address the waiting group.

"Okay. Pathology will provide additional answers in the next few days, but here's what we've got so far." He took a deep breath. "There's no doubt the skeleton submerged with the car. It belonged to someone five foot, seven inches tall. Based on the permanent teeth, no visible cavities, and other markers, I'm estimating an age of eighteen years. I see no evidence of blunt-force or blade trauma, which might rule out foul play. However, it's too early to make that determination. This individual experienced a broken right leg, a tibial fracture, much earlier in life—around ten years of age, it appears. Our next step will be to develop a biological profile to confirm age, sex, stature, and possibly ancestry."

He paused before dropping the bombshell: "However, one thing I can tell you today, for sure, is that this skeleton did *not* belong to Grant Dorrance Hutchinson."

Astonished, Tom—always quiet and thoughtful, known for considering his words before speaking—blurted, *"How do you know?"*

"Because it was a young woman," Dr. Walker replied.

The Sheriff was, as always, unfazed. "Okay," he said, turning to Meg. "Mr. Hutchinson's remains aren't in the car, so that leaves the pond. How about letting the muddy silt die down and then swimming a few laps along the bottom?"

"I'd love to," Meg said, winking at Suzanne and Kathy.

Over the next ninety minutes, Meg combed the pond's floor, swimming a grid of north–south and east–west laps, crisscrossing the underwater basin with a submersible spotlight that threw a bright, wide-angle beam across the silty bottom. She prodded the floor with a long plastic wand too, careful not to stir up the muck too much. But nothing turned up. "Except for a few animal bones," she reported. "Sorry."

"Don't be," the sheriff replied. "Mr. Hutchinson must have walked out—or someone carried him out." He paused for effect. "*If* he was ever in there."

"That never crossed my mind," Kathy whispered.

"Me neither," Suzanne whispered back. "We were all so excited about the possibility of solving the Hutchinson cold case that we got way ahead of ourselves. Not our best detective work," she added ruefully.

Tom chuckled. "You know what Dad always says: 'Be persuaded by your evidence, not by your hypothesis.'"

After Meg completed her survey, Tom, who had worn swimming trunks under his shorts, swam across the pond. He stepped out of the water on the far side and climbed to the top of the slope, seeking a vantage point from which to view the miner's track. As far as he could see, it meandered across the high desert, traveling in a northerly direction, everywhere rough and cluttered with debris. At some point, he realized, the route would have to run into County Road 10—the same highway that connected Prescott to Skull Valley.

Interesting.

"Dad, I feel embarrassed," Suzanne said. "A young woman? I mean, that was the *last* thing I expected to hear. I realized I'd failed to keep an open mind."

It was later that evening before the four young sleuths met with the Chief in the Jacksons' living room.

"Me too," Pete said, chomping on an apple. "Big surprise. Huge."

"Don't feel bad," the Chief replied. "In crime solving, we're often attached to our first ideas. Believe me, I've been there."

"So what happened to Mr. Hutchinson?" Tom asked. "And who was *she,* the unfortunate girl trapped inside the car?"

"And who penned the treasure map?" Kathy asked. "That's not just one mystery, *but three.*"

"Three, hmm," Pete said. "Maybe there were *three* people in the car, and two of them escaped."

"Why not four?" his sister bugged. He ignored the dig.

"No clue yet," the Chief said. "The sheriff will search missing-persons reports from around the same period. He's just hoping that the skeleton belongs to a local girl, otherwise . . ." He shook his head.

"Nothing makes sense," Suzanne mused aloud. "If Grant Hutchinson survived and walked away, the world would know, right?"

"Sure, you'd think so," the Chief replied. His eyes took on a faraway look. "On the other hand, lots of people disappear and they're never seen again, for multiple reasons that we can't even guess. And sometimes an individual reappears decades later, alive and well."

"There is something odd running through my mind," Kathy said.

"What's that?" the Chief asked.

"Well, if we are correct that Hutchinson himself was the 'treasure,' then whoever wrote that note believed Grant Dorrance Hutchinson was still in the water—for decades."

"Oh boy," Tom said. "You're right. That is strange, isn't it?"

"Remember, we're building on suppositions here," the Chief reminded.

"Right," Kathy chimed in. "But *if* the lady who drew the map was present when the car was driven or pushed into the water . . ."

"Then there's a good chance *two* people walked out of that pond," Suzanne finished her thought.

"In which case, I'm right again," Pete said as he poked his sister in the side.

"Or they weren't there to begin with," Tom said. "We just don't know. It's mystifying."

The Chief grinned. "That's why we call them mysteries."

"Do we have your permission to poke around this one?" Suzanne asked. "*We* found the skeleton—we'd like to follow up."

"I think so," the Chief said. He loved to encourage his home-grown mystery hunters, and especially the twins who were on a path to future careers in law enforcement. So far, they had shown every interest in following his footsteps. "Just let Sheriff McClennan know—he doesn't like surprises."

"Okay!" the foursome shouted in unison. They all shared a similar thought.

We're on it.

6

A COLD CASE

The Thursday morning edition of *The Daily Pilot* landed on the Jacksons' driveway with a familiar thud. Tom raced out to grab it, reading the headlines on the way back into the house.

"Hey, Suzie," he yelled, "Heidi Hoover got her scoop!"

His sister sprinted down the stairs, two at a time.

The lead headline shouted, "Missing heir's car found!" A subhead read, "Woman's skeleton recovered." The gripping story led off, "Grant Dorrance Hutchinson, the only son of Prescott's wealthiest family, disappeared in 1970, together with his new fire-engine-red Dodge Super Bee. The mystery lingered on for half a century before four Prescott High students discovered the car buried in six feet of water, a few miles from Skull Valley."

There was a photo of the foursome, arm in arm, grinning as they posed in front of the Dodge, the rusted hulk rescued and resting on dry land before it moved up onto the flatbed truck. The caption read, "Mystery searchers strike again."

Suzanne wanted to complain about her picture but didn't dare. Tom, she felt sure, would pounce.

"Nice story," the twins' mother, Sherri, said. She wrinkled her nose at the smell of fresh printer's ink. "Good for you guys—and Kathy and Pete too. Look, they even printed all your names in the article."

"Yeah," their father said, "but there wasn't much national coverage yesterday. Anyone figure out why?"

Tom replied, "Because Grant Hutchinson wasn't in that car."

"Right on."

"Well, we found *someone*," Suzanne said, sounding a little defensive.

"You sure did," the Chief said. "This thing will break open. It's only a matter of time."

The idea of half a century passing by without answers intrigued Sherri. "Boy, this story lay dormant for a long time. As if it were just waiting for the four of you to come along."

Suzanne's cell phone buzzed. "Hi, Kathy."

"Hi, yourself. Did you see that great pic?"

Suzanne groaned.

"THERE ARE PLENTY OF WAYS TO ATTACK THIS CASE," SUZANNE SAID. The mystery searchers had met later that same morning at the Jacksons'.

"Enlighten us," Pete challenged.

"Well, the Chief says Mr. Hutchinson had a sister," Tom said. "Let's start by finding her."

Kathy said, "I'm sure the Sheriff's Office is already searching for her."

"We'll ask him when he returns our call. What else?"

"Newspaper stories," Suzanne suggested. "Heidi mentioned that *The Daily Pilot* covered the story for the better part of a year."

They kicked things around for the next hour before the sheriff called. He appreciated their offer to help. "Sure, no problem. Call me if you run into anything interesting."

"One question we have," Suzanne said, "concerns Mr. Hutchinson's sister. Is she still alive?"

"We're looking for her," the senior officer replied. "We know her first name—it's Daisy—and that she'd be well into her sixties now. She was two years younger than her brother. Nothing else, yet." He thanked them again before disconnecting.

"Let's split up," Tom suggested. "Suzanne, you and Kathy attack the files at *The Daily Pilot*. We need to find everything possible about Grant Dorrance Hutchinson. What happened back in 1970? Maybe there's a hidden clue we can chase."

Pete said, "Meanwhile, we'll search for traces of Mr. Hutchinson's sister."

"Aye-aye, captain!" Kathy said, mock-saluting her brother. "Let's go, Suzie."

Kathy drove the Mustang downtown to the newspaper's corporate offices. On the way, Suzanne called Heidi Hoover.

"Hey, you," the affable reporter said.

"Hey, yourself," Suzanne said. "We're heading in your direction. Nice story this morning. Thank you."

"Yeah, my editors liked it too," Heidi replied with a little chuckle. "Thanks for the scoop."

Kathy called out "Hey!" in the background.

Suzanne switched her mobile to speaker phone mode.

"Hi, Kathy. Anything new?" the reporter asked.

"Not yet. But Sheriff McClennan gave us permission to dig into the mystery."

"Good for you guys. You're the best."

"Can we check through the newspaper's archives?" Suzanne asked.

"Sure. I'll meet you in the lobby."

Fifteen minutes later, the two girls found themselves ensconced in the archival center. The newspaper had been in operation since 1881 but stored much of its newer material in digital form. The earlier years' editions—everything pre-2000—were accessible only on microfilm: the bound volumes of the older copies, all printed on high-acid newsprint, were too fragile to examine. They had been transferred to an offsite climate-controlled storage facility for safety.

Each story was tagged with keywords, and one dedicated computer accessed the database. A day's entire edition was stored on a single microfilm. Finding the story was as easy as loading the film and scanning to the page number. But since the keyword-tagging system was not exhaustive, creative digging was the order of the day.

Heidi had spent a couple hours researching the Hutchinson case two days earlier. "I couldn't find anything you'd call a lead—neither could the police." She glanced at her screen to catch an in-coming message. "Gotta run, call me if you discover something interesting."

Kathy sat down at the keyboard. "Okay, I think I know where to start."

"Me too," Suzanne said. "Type in Grant Dorrance Hutchinson and then duck."

Kathy keyed in the words and hit *Enter*. "Oh, my gosh, one hundred and twenty-two entries."

Suzanne groaned out loud. "Let's get started. We'll be here for the rest of the day. Start with the first entry, then work up."

It hadn't occurred to either of them that Grant had attended the same high school they did. In 1969, a sports story lauded the young man for winning a first-place trophy in a swimming competition. Grant Dorrance Hutchinson soon materialized in front of them: a tall, lean, good-looking guy with an unruly mop of dark hair and a big grin stared back at them in black and white. He held the trophy high with strongly muscled arms.

"Oh, my word," Suzanne said. "What a tragedy. Whatever happened to this poor guy?"

It turned out that Grant—as they came to know more about him, they began calling him by his first name—had been quite the sports star. Not only did he excel at track but at football too. In his junior year at Prescott High, he was the team quarterback, taking the school to the quarterfinals in Phoenix. They lost, but even getting that far was a major victory.

"I'll bet that plaque is still hanging in the central hallway at school," Kathy said, picturing it.

Things changed in 1970. Grant moved from the sports page to the front page—and he stayed on it, off and on, for months.

"Grant Dorrance Hutchinson disappears!" read the next headline. There was a yearbook shot of a confident-looking young man, his hair slicked back. Another picture portrayed him beside his famous muscle car, one hand on its long hood with the twin scooped air intakes.

"Look at that big, handsome grin," Kathy said with a sadness in her voice.

A slew of headlines jumped off the page: "Prescott's leading family offers reward" . . . "Prescott City Police seeks help" . . . "FBI enters Hutchinson case" . . . "No break in Hutchinson investigation."

Two weeks later, in an ominous portent, the stories moved to page three. Now the headlines were more subdued: "No sign of Grant Dorrance Hutchinson" . . . "FBI explores kidnapping angle" . . . "Was Hutchinson's disappearance a kidnapping gone bad?"

Months slipped past. Sporadic updates appeared on page three, then five, and then eight. "Investigation at dead end," read one, and later headlines and reporting were similar. No clues. No breaks. And no sign of the missing heir and his fire-engine-red Dodge.

Anniversaries came and went: "Hutchinson still missing one year later" . . . "Five years since Hutchinson heir's disappearance." One story made the front page once again: "Ten years later, Hutchinson mystery persists."

There was even a brief twenty-year anniversary story, just a mention really, on page three . . . and then nothing.

Grant had vanished, seemingly forever—forgotten by time and banished from the pages of The Daily Pilot.

"Until today," Kathy noted.

"Yeah," Suzanne said, glancing over at her best friend. "Funny to think we were the catalyst."

Kathy giggled. "Isn't it? We moved Grant from nowhere to page one. No telling where that'll take us. Go back to that headline about the reward."

7

A SISTER SEARCH

The page-one article popped up on the screen with its headline, "Prescott's leading family offers reward."

It had appeared two weeks after the young man's disappearance. Beneath the headline was a black-and-white shot of a handsome middle-aged couple dressed in business attire and wearing pained expressions, backed up by half a dozen police officers in uniform.

Suzanne read the beginning out loud. "'Adolph and Meryl Hutchinson announced a reward for the return of their son, Grant Dorrance Hutchinson. 'We've established a $100,000 fund,' the boy's father said, 'for Grant's safe return. No questions asked. And if our boy is dead, we'll pay $50,000 for information leading to the recovery of his body.'"

"Oh, man, what a story," Kathy said, blinking back a tear. "Meryl's face is all wet."

Suzanne said, "What an unusual first name."

"Adolph?"

"No—Meryl. Never met anyone with that name."

"Me neither, but I like it. Has a nice ring to it."

An hour later, Kathy's cell phone buzzed. "Hey, you."

"Any luck?" Pete asked. Both set their cell phones on speaker.

"Nope, except we found out that Grant attended Prescott High," Suzanne said. "Nothing in the way of a clue."

"Wow, never figured on that," Tom said.

"He was big in sports too," Kathy said. "Took the football team to the league quarterfinals. I'll message you a pic of Grant now."

"You're calling him by his first name?" Tom asked.

"Why not? After all this research, it's almost as if we know the guy. Like he came back to life!"

Pete whistled. He was a running back on the same team, half a century later. "The quarterfinals? He must have been better than good. Hey, I just received the pic. That's him? I'll bet he was popular with the girls."

"He'd be popular with me," Kathy quipped.

"How are you guys doing?" Suzanne asked. "Anything on Daisy Hutchinson?"

Tom replied, "Yeah, we found something interesting. Meet us at the Shake Shop and we'll fill you in."

"Can you search Daisy's name while you're in the archives?" Pete asked. "See if she pops up."

"Sure," Kathy replied. "Like what, for example?"

"Like why she disappeared too."

IT WAS TRUE. WORKING TOGETHER AT THE BRUNELLIS' HOUSE AS THEY searched the internet, Tom and Pete had managed to find exactly zero traces of Daisy Hutchinson.

First, she had no online presence. No sign of her on Facebook, Instagram, Twitter, LinkedIn—nothing.

"Not surprising considering her age," Tom said.

"I dunno," Pete replied. "Lots of older people are on social media, especially Facebook." But not Daisy.

"Wait a sec," Tom suggested. "Let's try to find out her *married* name. All that information is available."

They logged onto the site for the Clerk of the Superior Court, which maintains all civil, domestic, and probate records for Yavapai County. They found Daisy's birth certificate, but no marriage, divorce or death certificates. Or anything else, for that matter.

"She might have died in a different state," Tom thought aloud, after another half-hour had slipped away with no results.

"Well, we're cooked if she did," Pete surmised. "I mean, how would we find *that*?"

"Just saying," Tom said. "It's possible . . . anything's possible."

"We need city records," Pete suggested. "Let's call Bill Holden."

Bill was Prescott's city engineer, the man who had aided them in one of their earlier cases, the hunt for the ghost in the county courthouse. Along the way, he had become a good friend.

Bill answered his phone on the first ring. "Hey, guys, great to hear from you. What's happening?"

"Bill, we're working a new mystery. Can we get check over some City Hall records?" Pete asked.

"You bet. I read about that car you found—great find! Come on down—I'll take you right in."

"Thanks."

Half an hour later, the boys were pouring through city records, looking for any trace of Daisy Hutchinson.

Her name showed up in a citywide census record from 1960, listed as "daughter," born two years after her brother. Fifteen years later another census occurred, recording the only residents at 1434 Brody Street as Adolph and Meryl Hutchinson—no Daisy.

"Property tax records next," Tom said. They searched, beginning in 1970, right through the current year.

"So she never bought a house in Prescott," Pete said.

"No, wait a sec." An idea had formed in Tom's mind. "Is it possible her parents purchased a home for her? I mean, it could make sense, right?"

"You bet it could. They were loaded. Let's check."

Thirty minutes later, Pete shouted, "Got it! The address, 1394 Brody Street, is just a block away from the family home. I'll bet anything Daisy lives there. And look, it's *still* in her parents' name."

Tom sat straight up. "After all this time?"

LATE THAT AFTERNOON, THE FOURSOME GATHERED AT THE SHAKE Shop. An unusual summer heat hung over the city as the girls enjoyed refreshing ice-cold chocolate milkshakes. Kathy, always a weight watcher, ordered a small one.

"Hi, guys, any luck?" she called out as the boys walked over to the outside picnic table.

"Yeah, we think so," Pete replied.

"Daisy Hutchinson keeps a low profile," Tom said, sitting down across from his sister. "But we think she's living a block away from the homestead."

Pete said, "Turns out the owners of her residence are her parents."

"Well, that's weird enough," Suzanne said.

"Weird? Why?"

"Her parents died in a car accident in Europe, back in 1981," Kathy replied. "Why wouldn't she have changed ownership records —legally register it in her own name?"

"No clue," Tom replied. "But just think—they never laid eyes on Grant again."

"Man, that's tough," Pete said. He ordered two large shakes— vanilla for Tom, chocolate for himself—from a passing waiter.

Suzanne flipped over a sheet of paper in front of her. "Here's a shot of Daisy taken at her parents' huge funeral." In the photo, a tall, slim woman with long, dark hair wore a black veil that failed to hide a face in mourning.

"Whoa," Tom said. "So at that point she would seem to be all alone in the world."

"Anything else?" Pete asked.

"Yes, and it's big too," Kathy said.

"Remember what Heidi told us?" Suzanne asked. She flipped over a copy of a newspaper story dated October 20, 1971 with the headline "Hutchinson kidnapping foiled." She read beginning aloud: "'Daisy Hutchinson, the only surviving child of Adolph and Meryl Hutchinson, beat off a kidnapping attempt late on Friday night in the family's open garage. An unknown man attempted to abduct Miss Hutchinson as she exited her vehicle. She reported to police that she screamed and kicked her assailant before a neighbor raced over to help, at which point the man fled. Miss Hutchinson further reported that the kidnapper had lost his hooded mask in the struggle and that she managed to get a good look at the perpetrator before he escaped in a van. Police are investigating and urge anyone with information that might lead to the attacker's arrest to come forward.'"

Adjacent to the article was a police sketch artist's portrait of the assailant based on Daisy's description, a head-and-shoulders view of an angry-looking young man, clean-shaven, with a snarling face and long, tangled dark hair.

The story continued: "'The Hutchinson family revealed for the first time that there had been another kidnapping attempt on Daisy three months earlier, which they had reported to local police. Our readers will also recall that her brother, Grant Dorrance Hutchinson, disappeared in 1970 and that his whereabouts remain a mystery to this day. The FBI continue to believe that the Hutchinson's son's disappearance was the result of 'a kidnapping gone bad.'"

Tom whistled. "A persistent criminal, maybe?"

"Assuming it was the same guy," Pete said, remembering the Chief's advice to the four friends not to jump to conclusions. The boys' shakes arrived. He passed the vanilla to Tom.

Suzanne said, "After that, Daisy's name appeared just once more in *The Daily Pilot*—after her parents' funeral, and never again."

"No darn wonder," Kathy said. "A bad guy targeted her, twice."

"Well," Tom said, deep in thought, "that sure explains why her house is still in her parents' name. I'll bet she's kept a low profile her whole life."

"So you're saying she's been hiding ever since the kidnapping attempts," Pete said. "No darn wonder. She probably figured someone targeted Grant too."

AFTER DINNER THAT NIGHT, THE MYSTERY SEARCHERS PARKED THEIR cars a block away from 1394 Brody Street. The sun had dropped, leaving behind an orange glow, but there was still plenty of light. Huge old elm trees stretched high above both sides of the street, creating a natural canopy through which the waning rays streaked. A million cicadas clicked and chirped.

The foursome meandered along the side opposite the beautiful Victorian-style home, with its steeply pitched roof, wide porch, bay windows, towers, and overhangs.

"It's an older home, for our town—turn of the century," Tom said.

A light burned inside the house on the second floor. Everywhere else was dark.

"Let's keep going," Pete suggested, "to 1434 Brody Street."

A block away, they walked past another Victorian-style mansion —the former home of Adolph and Meryl, where they had brought up their two children—a much larger residence with a wider front porch, set on a huge corner lot, but with similar period gingerbread details.

"So this was home to Grant and Daisy," Kathy said.

"They would have walked to Prescott High from here," Suzanne said.

"Sure they did," Pete said, "until the day that Super Bee arrived."

8

MISS DAISY HUTCHINSON

"We've located Grant's sister," Suzanne said on an early Friday morning call.

"Yeah, we found her too," the sheriff replied. "But she refuses to answer her phone, nor will she come to the front door and talk to our officers. My deputies tried three times. The neighbors claimed she's a complete recluse and has been for years. She stays out of sight."

Kathy said, "We're guessing we know why."

"Tell me."

"We found the story in the archives of *The Daily Pilot*," Suzanne explained. She briefly summarized the results of their research.

"Ah, sure, that makes sense," the sheriff said. "That was a long haul before my time. Your brother is thought to be dead from a kidnapping gone bad and then someone tried to kidnap *you*, twice. That's a lot of emotional trauma. No *wonder* she won't talk to us."

"Yes," Suzanne said, "We're betting those events turned her into a recluse. They must have been horrible experiences."

"Well, I sure can't fault her," the sheriff said, his voice sounding muffled as he took notes. They heard his fingers tapping on a keyboard.

"Sheriff," Pete asked, "why don't we try to see her today? Maybe she'll talk to us."

"Sure. It's worth trying. But I'd suggest Suzanne and Kathy make the attempt. Since Daisy Hutchinson is a recluse, there's no way she'll see all four of you. Plus, she might identify with the girls."

"Good advice," Kathy said. "Thank you."

"You're welcome. Keep me in the loop."

LATER THAT MORNING, THE GIRLS PARKED IN FRONT OF 1394 BRODY Street. They stepped out of the car and walked over to a low-slung white picket fence with a latched gate. Then they marched up the steps onto the wide porch and rang the front doorbell. Silence. They waited.

"The doorbell doesn't work," Kathy whispered.

Suzanne knocked. The sound of footsteps descending a stairwell occurred before the inside door opened. A middle-aged woman with gray hair and an immaculate maid's uniform stood on the other side of the screen. "May I help you?"

Kathy said, "We'd like to see Daisy Hutchinson."

"I'm sorry. *Miss* Hutchinson doesn't receive visitors." The maid began to close the door.

"We're the ones who found Grant's car," Suzanne said quickly. "Miss Hutchinson will want to talk to us."

There was a hesitation. The woman stared at them. "One moment, please."

The girls glanced at each other. Kathy shrugged. "Should be interesting."

The maid reappeared a minute later and unlocked the outside screen door. "Please follow me." *It worked.*

The girls stepped into an old Victorian entry hall that soared above them. They stepped over fine parquet floors, polished to gleaming, and admired the coffered ceilings. Competing odors greeted them—a stale smell born of doors and windows closed for too many years fought with the strong odor of freshly mopped floors.

The polite maid led them into a spacious front parlor with spotless antique furniture arranged around a fine octagonal Oriental carpet. "Please make yourselves comfortable. Miss Hutchinson will be down shortly. My name is Sarah. May I get you something to drink, water or tea?"

"Thank you," Suzanne replied. "Tea sounds great." Sarah disappeared down a hallway.

Minutes later, they heard footsteps on the stairwell just as Sarah arrived with the tea. A tall, striking, older woman with short, neatly styled gray hair entered the room. She wore a tailored, short-sleeved silk blouse, white with silver splotches, closed at her throat with a gold broach, and a long black skirt. Her piercing blue eyes searched their faces as she approached and extended a hand in greeting.

"I am Miss Daisy Hutchinson. Who are you?"

The two girls stood and shook hands, both noticing how Miss Hutchinson exuded self-confidence. They introduced themselves.

"Suzanne and Kathy," Miss. Hutchinson repeated. She sat down on a stiff-backed antique chair opposite her visitors. "Please, make yourselves comfortable."

The girls sat down together on an overstuffed sofa covered in elegant brocade.

"It was you who found Grant's car," Miss Hutchinson began. "How?"

The woman gasped when Suzanne explained about the hand-drawn treasure map ending with the big "X" over the water.

"Tell me," she said, "what did the treasure map say?"

"I've reread the directions so many times, I've memorized them," Suzanne said. She recited them aloud: "'Take Iron Springs Road (county road 10) to Skull Valley. Turn left on Copper Basin Road, 6.3 miles. Turn right to switch to the secondary road, go 1.3 miles. Park, and walk left along the dry creek road for half a mile. Watch for the water! Please help, whoever you are. Thank you.'"

Silence.

Miss Daisy Hutchinson's eyes bored into Suzanne with a strange intensity. After a few moments, she spoke. "What an unusual ending. 'Please help, whoever you are . . . Thank you.' What could that mean?"

Suzanne said, "My father is Prescott's chief of police, and my mother is a social worker. They believe those words are a cry of guilt."

Miss Hutchinson looked away for a few seconds. The two girls sipped on their cooling tea.

"Do you have any idea why the car would be out near Skull Valley?" Kathy asked.

"I don't."

"Do you know about the skeleton?"

"Yes, I can read."

"Any clue who she might have been?"

"None. Grant was a popular boy. He had girlfriends and a lot more after Dad bought him that horrible car. But no one else disappeared from around here when Grant did . . . that we knew of."

Suzanne said, "There was a title above the map."

"A title? What did it say?"

"'My Treasure Map,'" Kathy said.

Miss Hutchinson repeated the words, almost in a whisper. "My . . . treasure . . . map." Her eyes watered before she turned away. She stared out through a large picture window and seemed to lose herself in thought for a full minute. Out front, the Chevy was visible under a gigantic elm tree that reached high across the street.

"Do those words mean anything to you?" Suzanne asked, breaking the spell.

Miss Hutchinson turned back. "I need to think about it. Why is it that you are poking into my family's life?"

The girls glanced at each other again before Kathy answered. "We work with our brothers and solve mysteries. We've solved others, and we'd like to take a shot at this one."

"This is a big mystery," Suzanne said. "Your brother's remains weren't in the car, nor could the police find any evidence that they were in the pond."

Miss Hutchinson searched their faces again. "The police and the FBI tried to solve the mystery of his disappearance in the past, and they came up empty. Please tell them to stay away and leave me alone."

"Can you think of *anything* that might help us?" Suzanne asked.

Miss Hutchinson stared at the girls intently before answering. "Not yet." Then she stood. "Thank you for finding Grant's car. I am most appreciative." She turned and walked away without saying another word, disappearing up the stairs.

Sarah, the ever-polite maid, returned seconds later. "Please follow me." She opened the front door. "Thank you for coming."

The girls stepped into the fresh air and locked eyes in astonishment. Kathy spoke first. "How strange was that? She just *walked* away."

"Well, she lives in a different world," Suzanne said. "What did she mean when she said, 'I need to think about it,' and 'Not yet?' What's that all about?"

"She knows *something*," Kathy said. "We lit a fire here, and something will come from it—I'm sure."

"I hope you're right," Suzanne said. "She's a very nice lady. And she's suffered a lot. I agree—sooner or later . . ."

"Better be sooner," Kathy said. "We haven't much to go on."

The girls called the sheriff and brought him up to date on their meeting.

"We feel positive she knows something," Suzanne said.

"And we'll stay in touch with her," Kathy added. "But she requested no contact from any police officers."

"Yeah, I figured as much," he replied. "In her books, we failed. More than once too. Hard to blame her."

9

AN INVITATION

The mail arrived at the Jacksons' later that same afternoon. Sherri waved to the friendly mailman as he departed before picking up the stack and flipping through. Then she deposited it on the entrance-way table and stepped back into her home office.

An hour passed before the twins returned home for dinner. Suzanne sorted through the stack of mail, looking for catalogs. Buried at the bottom was a small envelope—the same size as a thank-you card—addressed to Tom and Suzanne Jackson, without a return address.

Hmm, what's this, she wondered, opening the envelope and retracting a folded piece of paper. It read, in spidery cursive,

 There's something waiting for you at the pond.

"Tom!" she yelled upstairs.

He raced down, alarmed at the tone in his sister's voice. She held up the note with two fingers—"Read, don't touch." She knew her father would want it checked for fingerprints. Inwardly, she regretted tearing the envelope open without more thought.

"Oh, boy," Tom said, scanning the missive. "We've triggered someone, for sure."

The Chief and their mother soon gathered around the table with the twins.

"I don't like it," Sherri said with a worried frown. "Not at all. What does this mean?"

"It means another individual knows something about the fate of Grant Dorrance Hutchinson," Suzanne replied.

"And whoever that person is," Tom added, "he or she is sending a message."

The Chief stepped into the kitchen and returned with a ziplock sandwich bag. "Drop the note in here. The envelope too. I doubt whether he left fingerprints for us, but anything's possible."

"*He?* The writer is a he?" Suzanne asked, picking up first the note, then the envelope gingerly by one corner and slipping them into the open plastic bag at arm's length.

"Sure," Tom said. "Check out the handwriting. Likely masculine, I'd say. And the guy is older too—more shaky writing."

Suzanne moved in closer. "I see what you mean. What's he trying to tell us?"

Tom hesitated. "No clue. I can't imagine what we could have missed. Whatever the gentleman is referring to wasn't in the car *or* the pond."

"So a different kind of treasure," Sherri mused, "in the surrounding area."

"I don't think so, Mom," Suzanne stated in a firm voice. "The note says '*at* the pond,' not 'near the pond.'"

"Nor 'in the pond,'" Tom said

"Good point," the Chief said. "Well, there's one thing for sure: whoever this guy is, he knows where we live. Stay cautious."

"And I'll stay worried," their mother said, the corners of her mouth turning down.

"Oh, Mom, there's nothing to worry about," Suzanne said.

Or is there? she thought.

. . .

That evening, the four mystery searchers met to hammer out strategy. First up was the strange note.

"Well, we gotta make a return trip," Pete said. "This strange dude left a clue for us out there."

"Or it's nothing more than a practical joke," Tom surmised. "Some guy who read about the case in the paper and is just playing us. Either way, that has to be our next stop."

"Okay, we're all in," Suzanne agreed. "But no matter what, Grant Dorrance Hutchinson did not die in that swamp."

"Or if he did, someone carried him out," Kathy said.

"How likely is that?" Pete snapped.

"You haven't got a clue," Kathy snapped back, clearly irritated.

Suzanne interrupted the coming fray. "It's far more credible that he walked away—if he was ever there. Remember, we have no evidence proving anything."

"I agree," Tom said. "But how on earth *can* we prove he walked out? I mean, finding out what happened to Grant has to be our number-one goal."

"Easy," Kathy said brightly. "We find him."

That comment sent Pete into a fit of laughter that earned him a withering look from his sister. "Uh-huh. Fifty years later. Nothing to it. Sure."

"There's something else too," Suzanne said. "If we found the guy, he'd be in a world of trouble."

"No kidding," Tom said. "For starters, if he was the one who drove his car into the swamp. That could be manslaughter."

"Oh, boy," Pete said, "If Grant is alive, he might pay a heavy price for leaving that girl in the Dodge."

Silence reigned for a long moment. "Maybe he didn't leave her," Kathy said, breaking the interlude.

Pete stared at his sister. "What do you mean?"

"Maybe *she* left *him*."

"I don't get it."

"What else is new?"

"I do," Suzanne said, glancing at Kathy. "You're saying she died in the crash—or drowned."

"Right. And what if there wasn't a thing Grant could do? What then?"

"Like, if it was an accident? In that case, it wouldn't be manslaughter . . . or murder," Tom said.

"That's a welcome thought," Suzanne said.

"Nice idea, but I don't buy it," Pete said. "If Grant escaped, he would have called the cops. And don't forget: leaving the scene of an accident in which someone dies is, well, I don't know if it's a crime exactly, but it's still gotta be wrong."

"Right or wrong, he could be alive today," Kathy argued. "And we don't know the circumstances."

"The man hasn't reappeared in half a century," Pete said, refusing to surrender. "If he's still alive—and that's a big *if*—why has he been hiding so long?"

"No clue," Suzanne replied, "but it's at least *possible* he survived, isn't it? And if he is alive, how would we go about finding him?"

Tom grinned. "Well, there was no Internet in 1970. Things have changed since then, haven't they?"

10

A DESERT SURPRISE

The mystery searchers fleshed out Tom's idea—simple enough but requiring a little effort to pull it together. "It's more than possible that it'll work," Suzanne said eagerly. "Maybe even probable."

Kathy called Sheriff McClennan—they needed his approval. "I like it. So you'll post a picture of Grant Dorrance Hutchinson on social media and tell the world the man is missing and you're looking for him. You'll need a lot of 'shares,' but the results could be interesting."

Next, the twins enlisted their father's help.

"Dad, do you have a colleague who could create an age-progressed image of Grant Hutchinson. If he's alive, we need a good idea of what he would look like today."

The Chief called in a favor, prevailing on a well-known forensic artist in Phoenix who sometimes worked as a consultant for Arizona police departments and was famous for the accuracy of her work. She requested a range of photographs, including immediate family. The Brunellis emailed her a clean yearbook shot of Grant taken in 1970 that they found reproduced in the *Pilot*, plus other newspaper pictures from the paper's archives: the iconic pic of the young man leaning against his prized muscle car, the photo of his parents beside the reward presser, and the shot of his sister at the funeral.

ON SUNDAY MORNING, THE TWO FAMILIES ATTENDED MASS AT ST. Francis Church. Afterward, they gathered together for their customary Sunday brunch. No one loved Arizona's famous Mexican food more than the foursome.

Hot and spicy tamales, tacos, chimichangas, enchiladas, and bean salads were all wolfed down over the next hour.

While the parents caught up with one another, the mystery searchers plotted quietly—between bites—at the other end of the table.

LATER THAT DAY, THE JACKSON-BRUNELLI TEAM WAS BACK ON THE miner's track, dressed for hiking and on their way to the "swamp," as Tom insisted on calling it.

"The good news is that we don't have to swim in it again," Suzanne said as they trudged along the route.

Kathy couldn't agree more. "Whatever's out there, we need to find it before anyone else does."

"As if anyone else goes out here," Pete said.

"Well, something's going on," Suzanne said. "I can't imagine what we missed."

"We'll spread out and circle the swamp to start when we get there," Tom suggested.

The foursome lapsed into silence. They hadn't gone far, walking for just twenty minutes along, when—

Bam! . . . Bam! . . . Bam! . . . Bam! . . . Three or four seconds passed between each shot.

"Uh-oh," Suzanne said, freezing in her tracks. "What's *that* all about?"

"Four rifle shots," her brother replied. "Quite a distance from where we are. Desert target practice, I'd guess. There's lots of that out here."

"I don't like it," Kathy declared, glancing backwards.

"It's behind us," Pete said with a shrug. "Way back there. Nothing to worry about." He shifted his backpack into a more comfortable position.

The high desert heat closed in on them as the temperature edged up. By now, the route was quite familiar. They dodged rocks, boulders, and dead trees, trailing the giant tire tracks of the wrecker. Kathy kept a sharp eye open for snakes.

"Okay, we're here," Pete hollered as they descended toward the ravine. The pond spread before them. "What now?"

"Circle around," Suzanne said. "Scout the area and look for—"

There was a loud *crack!* and a whizzing sound. Pete instantly knew what was happening. "Someone's shooting at us!" He grabbed Kathy's arm and hightailed it out of the ravine and into the high desert. The twins zig-zagged right behind them.

Crack! A bullet struck a nearby rock wall with a loud *ping!*

"Spread out!" Tom shouted, racing behind Suzanne. "Get as far away from here as possible!"

There was another *crack!* and a bullet whizzed past them. The foursome circled a huge bluff, making their way to its far side at high speed, ducking and weaving before reaching what they hoped was safety. They stopped, panting hard, bent over, and trying to catch their breath.

"What on earth—?" Kathy asked between gasps.

"*That's* what was waiting at the pond," Tom said, thinking back to the letter.

"We gotta get out of here, fast!" Pete urged.

"You're right." Tom's mind raced. "Into the desert, otherwise this lunatic could trap us."

Suzanne was furious, her face beet red. "Not—liking—this—"

She reached into her backpack and grabbed her cellphone, touching 911. "There's no cell service out here. We've got to close the distance to the main road."

"What about snakes?" Kathy asked, her eyes scouring the ground.

"The human kind are much more dangerous," Pete replied. "Follow one another in single file and spread out."

A long, grueling hour passed in virtual silence before the welcome sight of the gravel road—with the bright white Chevy parked to the side—loomed in the distance. There was no further sign of the shooter.

Suzanne checked her cell phone for the umpteenth time. "We've got cell service!" The foursome cheered.

They reached the roadway and raced over to the car. That's when Tom spotted their next big hurdle. "Hey! The tires are flat!"

There was a collective gasp.

"All *four* of them?" Suzanne asked. She couldn't believe her eyes.

Pete bent down and examined the front left. "This one's got a bullet hole in it."

"So does this one," Kathy said, checking the rear passenger side.

"Oh, man," Tom said. "Not good. That explains the first four shots we heard."

Pete said, "Okay. Great. While we were hiking, the shooter blew our tires away."

The Chief answered his emergency phone on the second ring. "Dad, we've got a problem," Suzanne said.

AN HOUR LATER, COPPER BASIN ROAD—THE DESERTED STRETCH JUST eight miles from Skull Valley—experienced an unusual amount of traffic. Two deputies had arrived, followed by Sheriff McClennan and the Chief, all in separate vehicles and parked in a line behind the Chevy. Soon, a flatbed tow truck rumbled along and backed up to the disabled vehicle.

"It was a .30–30 Winchester," one deputy said, holding a spent and misshapen flat-nosed bullet between two fingers.

"So why?" the Chief asked the four aspiring detectives. "Why do *you* think someone would do this?"

"Well," Suzanne replied, "it's obvious he wasn't trying to hurt us."

"If he wanted to bump us off …" Pete said. He didn't have to finish the thought.

"He was just trying to scare us," Kathy said, "to keep us away from the pond—"

"And off the case," Tom concluded.

"I think you're right," Sheriff McClennan said, nodding. "Nothing would have prevented him from shooting you out here in the middle of nowhere." He pointed out into the desolate high desert. "From his well-hidden vantage, you were totally vulnerable. You just received a warning."

"We all did," the Chief said.

"That's reassuring," Suzanne said dryly.

"You're mucking around in the Hutchinson mystery, and someone knows something about it," the Chief said. "Somehow, he perceives you as a threat—and a greater threat than we are, local law enforcement."

"How does he know about us?" Suzanne asked.

"*The Daily Pilot* printed all your names," the sheriff said.

Her face colored. "Well, *duh*."

"Must be the same person who sent that note to draw us out here. And he knows us well enough to bet that we would be coming out today," Pete said.

"He wanted to fire you up—quick too," the Chief said. "And it worked, right?"

"So I'm sure he was watching our house too," Tom said.

"No one followed you out here?" the sheriff asked.

"Not a chance," Tom replied. "We were the only ones on this road—for miles."

"Yeah, he had you pegged and where you were heading," the Chief said. "And he knew his way out here. Whoever this person is, he's well informed. Too bad he didn't leave fingerprints on the invitation."

"Oh, boy," Kathy said to the twins. "Imagine the guy spying on you. *Creepy.*"

"Imagine the guy *shooting* at us!" Pete retorted.

"We need to find him first before he makes another move," Tom said.

"We'll do just that," Suzanne said. Her emotions had run the gamut—from fear, through worry, to indignation, and now, anger. "It'll take more than a few random shots to shake us off this case."

"Make sure you don't say that to your mother," the Chief warned.

DO YOU KNOW ME?

On Monday morning—one week after the intriguing cry for help fell from the pages of *Wuthering Heights*—stunning images of Grant Dorrance Hutchinson appeared in Suzanne's inbox as she sat chewing over the evidence with Kathy.

In her cover email, the forensic artist explained her approach: "Thanks for the photos. Since Grant died in 1970 at age seventeen, I created a 'close age' image to the present day. I aged Grant by giving him a receding hairline and styling his remaining hair, which I also grayed, in an age-appropriate manner for today. He might also be completely bald by now, but since his father had thick hair late in life (and even though male-pattern baldness can be inherited from either parent), I've split the difference and shown Grant balding considerably—but not bald. I also dropped the tip of his nose, lengthened his earlobes, and turned slight depressions in his teenage skin into wrinkles—all normal aspects of aging. The turned-down corners of his mouth represent aging due to loss of skin and muscle tone. I've given you three options for facial hair: clean shaven, with gray stubble, and with a full beard and mustache."

"Oh, my gosh," Kathy said. "These are as good as photographs. You can see it's the same guy, but—wow."

"Check out those eyes," Suzanne exclaimed. "And those ears. He's the spitting image of his father. It's amazing."

Gray strays of hair folded across Grant's pate, replacing his once well-known teenage seventies mop. His eyes still twinkled, and his chin appeared identical in the clean-shaven image to the way it looked in his high school photo. His cheeks sagged, but the nose matched that of his elegant and still-attractive sister.

"A little longer than hers," Kathy said, giggling. "But can't you just tell that Daisy and Grant are siblings?"

The two girls put Suzanne's mobile on speaker for a big thank-you phone call to the artist. "You're welcome," she replied. "Send me a pic if you find him. I'm curious to know how close I got."

"We will!" Suzanne said before saying goodbye.

"Not if," Kathy said after the call. "*When.*"

Later, when the boys saw the drawings, they were ecstatic. "Okay," Tom said. "I bet we couldn't get any closer. Now for the next step."

PETE AND KATHY'S FATHER, JOE, WAS A WELL-KNOWN MAGAZINE publisher who specialized in history and enjoyed a worldwide readership, in print and online. The siblings managed their father's website and prepared all the graphics.

Given their expertise, it fell to the brother-and-sister team to create a new, eye-catching graphic featuring Grant Dorrance Hutchinson for online posting. Kathy started by scanning the high school yearbook photograph of the handsome young man. Beside it, she dropped in the age-progressed images. Centered above the four pictures appeared the headlines:

Please share! Please share! Please share!
Do You Know Me?

MY NAME IS GRANT DORRANCE HUTCHINSON
AND I'VE BEEN MISSING FOR HALF A CENTURY

Below the images was the story they hoped would unlock the secrets of the boy's disappearance:

ON AUGUST 1, 1970
GRANT DORRANCE HUTCHISON'S
DODGE SUPER BEE SUBMERGED IN A POND
NEAR SKULL VALLEY, ARIZONA.
RECENT EVENTS SUGGEST HE
MIGHT HAVE SURVIVED THE INCIDENT.
IF YOU HAVE SEEN THIS MAN,
PLEASE CALL THE
YAVAPAI COUNTY SHERIFF'S OFFICE:
OR KATHY:

She typed in the two phone numbers. "Okay, finished."

"Why should you get the calls?" Pete said, even though he didn't care.

"Because I'm doing most of the work, that's why," Kathy replied, tossing her head.

They emailed the completed post to the twins, Sheriff McClennan, the Chief, and Heidi Hooper at *The Daily Pilot*.

Kathy's elation shone. "The fun is just about to begin."

THAT AFTERNOON, THE TWINS PICKED UP THE CHEVY—SPORTING FOUR brand-new, gleaming black tires.

"Nice ride," Tom said.

"Very. You realize we'll have to pay Dad back."

"*Aargh*," Tom groaned.

In the evening, the mystery searchers released the post the Brunellis had created on every major social media site, tagged with searchable terms such as *PrescottArizonahistory*, *missingpersonscoldcase*, and more. Facebook, Instagram, Pinterest, Twitter, and a number of chatroom sites were all touched in one way or another. Each of the four had their own favorite sites, together with long lists of friends.

Heidi called. "I'll try to get it on the front page, but I can't control placement. It's a great human-interest story and part of Prescott's history. It'll go on our newspaper's website and the wire services, so there's a good chance other papers will pick it up."

"By this time tomorrow, it'll reach humongous numbers of people," Suzanne said.

"Tens of thousands," Tom declared. "Even more. I've studied releases like this. They're phenomenal. This thing could go viral."

"We'd better not surprise Miss Hutchinson," Kathy suggested. "Let's visit her tomorrow."

"Surprise her?" Suzanne said. But it wasn't a question. "She'll be well and truly shocked."

Tom fell noticeably silent.

"What's up, bro?" his sister asked.

"I've been thinking about the treasure map—about how it ended up at St. Vincent de Paul."

"What about it?"

"Well, the lady died—at least, that's what the attached note said. But it's odd that someone dropped the donation off in the middle of the night."

"That's a fact," Pete said.

"Whoever that person is," Tom continued, "he or she must have been close to the mysterious woman. Close enough to handle something precious to her."

"That makes sense," Suzanne said. "Those books *were* special. Lots of classics—some valuable editions too."

"And if we can find whoever handled the drop-off," Tom said, "that same person could lead us to the author of the treasure map."

"Suzie, does the thrift store have security cameras?" Kathy asked.

"Well . . ." Suzanne hesitated. "There's a security *system*, for sure."

"Whoa, I should have thought of that," Tom said.

"You're not kidding, hotshot," his sister retorted. "You're the tech guy."

He ignored the dig. "And since they have a system, I'd guess they've deployed cameras. Maybe we can see footage of whoever dropped those books off."

"Super!" Pete said. "That's our next stop."

1 2

A WILD GOOSE CHASE

The first order of business on Tuesday was a nine o'clock visit to Miss Hutchinson. The girls stepped up the wide porch, and Kathy knocked—loudly.

A minute passed before Sarah appeared, greeting them with a cheerful, "Good morning."

"Hello," Suzanne began. "We need to talk to Miss Hutchinson. We have something important to tell her."

This time there was no hesitation. Sarah unlocked the outside screen door. "Follow me, please. May I offer you some tea?"

She led the girls into the same front parlor as before. Ten minutes later, tea arrived—just ahead of Miss Hutchinson. The elegant lady swept in, dressed once again in a long, beautiful dark skirt and a silk blouse. The girls rose to greet her.

"Hello, again," she said, offering her hand and a half-smile. "Please, sit down and enjoy your tea. I understand you have some-thing to tell me."

"Yes, we do," Suzanne said. She paused, searching for the right words. "Miss Hutchinson, we all know that your brother's remains weren't in the car, nor was there any trace of him at the bottom of the pond. It's quite certain he didn't drown in the accident—if it was an accident."

"So we figured he might still be alive, living somewhere else in the world," Kathy said.

"On the surface, that makes no sense," Miss Hutchinson demurred. "If he survived, we'd know about it."

"Yes," Suzanne said, "one would think so. But stranger things have happened."

"So in the happy event that he *is* still alive," Kathy continued, "we came up with an idea to find him. Suzanne's father located a forensic artist in Phoenix and asked her to create age-progressed drawings of your brother."

"If Grant is alive today, we wanted to see how he might look," Suzanne said, picking up the thread. "So we sent the artist a variety of photos gathered from *The Daily Pilot*, including his yearbook shot. She created her work using those images as guideposts."

Suzanne opened a folder and extracted a sheet of paper—an 8x11 full-color printout showing the images of Grant executed by the forensic artist.

Miss Hutchinson, accepting the flyer in one hand, gasped audibly. Her other hand flew to her mouth. Her eyes watered. A long moment of silence ensued while she tried to compose herself.

"Sarah," she called out weakly. The ever-polite maid appeared from nowhere. "Please bring me a tissue."

Miss Hutchinson breathed, hard, before glancing back at the two girls. "It's interesting, I can see our father *and* our mother in him, but he looks more like Dad."

"We noticed the resemblance between you and your brother too," Suzanne said.

"Yes," she said, "I agree."

Sarah handed her a tissue. Miss Hutchinson wiped her eyes.

"There's something else," Kathy said. "We created material for social media platforms and released it last night."

Suzanne passed over a second sheet of paper. Miss Hutchinson fell silent as she studied the page.

"I learned about the pond many years ago," she said at length. "When I read that you had found his car, it shocked me that his remains weren't there."

"You—you *knew* about the pond?" Suzanne stammered. "Years ago? Whatever do you mean, Miss Hutchinson?"

In reply, she stood and walked out of the room. "I'll be right back."

Suzanne and Kathy glanced at each other with raised eyebrows. Neither said a word.

Miss Hutchinson returned a minute later and thrust a folded piece of paper toward them. Suzanne opened the sheet to find that it was a letter, brittle with age. The girls sat beside each other, and read a missive dated September 15, 1981:

DEAR MISS HUTCHINSON—YOUR BROTHER GRANT DIED IN A TERRIBLE *accident the same night he disappeared. His car went into a gigantic pond in the desert and he drowned. From Skull Valley go right on Copper Basin Road, 6.3 miles. Turn right to switch right to the secondary road, go 1.3 miles. Turn left and drive north along the dry creek road for half a mile. The water appears suddenly, be careful. I have kept this terrible secret for so long. I'm so sorry, this has haunted me ever since. Please forgive me.*

"THAT HANDWRITING," SUZANNE SAID, HER VOICE RISING. "WE'VE seen it before—on the treasure map."

"You bet we have," Kathy said firmly. "It's so recognizable—and the wording of the directions is darn near identical too. But there's no shakiness in this writing."

"Oh, that's interesting," Miss Hutchinson said, startled. "So you think the same person drew your map? That means she's still alive."

"She was when she drew it," Kathy said. "But whoever dropped the books off at the thrift store left a note. It read, 'The lady died.'"

"Oh, I see." A look of disappointment crossed Miss Hutchinson's face. "She had secrets she could have shared."

"You received this letter back in 1981."

"Yes, one week after my parents died,"

"Wow," Suzanne said. "By then the roadbed was impassable—the hundred-year-flood had dumped rocks and dead trees everywhere, and the mystery woman must have known it. It's obvious she had returned to the pond since—since the . . . incident. At least once."

"Did you go out there?" Kathy asked.

"I sure did. And I searched multiple roads too. There wasn't a drop of water for miles. Every one of the miners' routes was littered with debris and the instructions didn't add up. I thought it was someone's idea of a bizarre joke—until your story appeared in *The Daily Pilot.*"

"That makes no sense," Kathy said. "It was three years after the floods. Wouldn't the pond have been overflowing?"

Suzanne was busy scanning the letter. "Wait a sec. It says, 'From Skull Valley go right on Copper Basin Road'—that's wrong! From Skull Valley, you go left—not right." She raised a hand to her forehead. "That little error sent you in the exact opposite direction, miles off course."

"Wow," Kathy said softly. "The mysterious writer made a huge mistake."

"Oh, my goodness," Miss Hutchinson replied. She paused, sighing deeply, but the error didn't seem to rattle her. So many years had passed . . . "One thing the letter *does* say is that Grant died. But if that was true, why weren't his remains found?"

She sighed again, with a shudder, and looked away. "Nothing makes sense. It never has."

13

SURVIVAL

Meanwhile, the boys had made their way to the St. Vincent de Paul Thrift Store. They brought Mrs. Otto up to date on their adventures since the discovery of the treasure map.

"Oh, yes," she replied. She pushed her glasses up to the bridge of her nose. "I read about finding that car. And Suzanne called and told me about the skeleton. Imagine something like that starting—right here in our store!"

"Well," Tom explained, "we're trying to find the individual who donated those books. Suzanne said the boxes appeared on your loading dock during the night."

Mrs. Otto's face lit up as she tried her best to be helpful. "That's correct."

Tom asked, "Is there a security camera overlooking the dock?"

"Why, yes," Mrs. Otto replied. "There surely is."

Pete rubbed his hands together in glee. "Great! Video footage?"

"Well, video *stills*, I think they're called," Mrs. Otto replied.

"How long is the footage stored?" Tom asked.

"Two weeks."

Tom breathed a sigh of relief. "Okay, we're on time."

"We'll still have them," she said, pursing her lips. "Let's go over to my computer."

Minutes later, the boys were scanning through security stills on Mrs. Otto's desktop monitor. They fast-forwarded through the evening, past midnight, and into the early morning hours of the known date. Nothing. That changed as the day/time stamp in the lower right corner of the screen ticked over to MONDAY JUNE 3 03:28:00 AM.

"Here he comes," Pete said, moving closer to the monitor. Headlights had lit up a still.

Tom hit *Play*.

In the eerie yellowish glare cast by a single security light mounted over the store's back door, the boys watched as a dark-colored sedan drew up to the loading dock. The camera pointed straight out from above the door, capturing the driver's side of the vehicle.

"No way to see the license plates," Tom murmured.

A tall, slim man—he had to be in his late sixties or even older—wearing a short-sleeved shirt, jeans, and running shoes stepped out of the car and opened the rear passenger door. Then he popped the trunk with his key fob.

"Gotta be him," Pete said.

"He's a much older guy," Tom noted. "Thin face with sunken checks and a frown. No glasses and not much hair, either."

It took the man two minutes of struggling to unload ten heavy boxes—three from the back seat and the balance from the trunk—one after another, piling them onto the dock. Each time he plunged inside the car, he disappeared from camera view for several seconds. Then, his job complete, he slammed the trunk down and closed the back door before climbing back into the driver's seat. He zipped away.

Tom called out to Mrs. Otto, who was busy working the cash register. "How many boxes came in that night?"

"Ten," she replied. "Good books too. Tell Suzanne we sold that copy of *Wuthering Heights* this morning. She'll be pleased."

Pete scanned back and forth through the security footage to get the closest, clearest shot of the man. He froze the image and hit *Print*, three copies. Behind them a printer-copier started up, spitting out paper.

Tom walked over to Mrs. Otto and held the captured photo up to her. "Have you ever seen this guy before?"

She adjusted her glasses and tilted her head, staring at the picture for a few moments. "Never."

Tom used his cell phone to capture the printout's digital image. He forwarded it to the girls.

"What now?" Pete asked.

"Well, without a license plate number," Tom replied, "there's no way to identify him unless we somehow find someone who recognizes his face, so let's reverse things. We know—or at least we believe—the woman who owned all these books died. Let's parse through the obituaries at *The Daily Pilot* and search for a clue. Maybe *she* can lead us to *him*."

"If we find her, we don't need him," Pete said.

"Sure we do," Tom argued. "Think about it. He's the only person in this case who's skulking around in the middle of the night, hiding his identity—and that of the woman who owned the books. For some unknown reason, he's protecting her involvement in the tragedy."

"Or he's directly involved," Pete figured. "Like, he doesn't want Grant found, dead or alive. That might make sense."

"Anything's possible," Tom said. "And there's something else going through my brain. I'll bet anything he's the shooter."

"Oh, wow! That's a thought. What makes you think so?"

"It's a process of elimination," Tom replied. "Whoever this guy is, it seems he's the only one with secrets to hide."

Pete's cell phone buzzed. "We received Tom's message," Kathy said. She put him on speaker so Suzanne could hear. "Is he the one who dropped off the donation?"

"He sure is," Pete replied, feeling proud of their success. "And Tom thinks the same guy must be the shooter."

"The shooter!" Suzanne exclaimed in the background. "Well, I hope you're right. It would help to identify him before he comes back for more."

Pete asked, "How about you? Any response to the posting?"

"Oh, for sure," Kathy said, excited that her idea had paid off. Her cell had already buzzed three times that day. "Two kooks and a nut," she reported with a laugh. "This sort of thing sure brings them out, doesn't it? None of them had any connection with the family. One woman asked me about a reward. Can you *believe* it?"

Meanwhile, Suzanne had messaged Sheriff McClennan with an overview of the girls' meeting with Miss Hutchinson. He replied, *Thanks—Have received two calls on the post. Nothing.* Suzanne held up her cell phone so Kathy could read the text.

"Make that five nuts," she quipped to the boys.

On Wednesday morning, a reporter from Los Angeles called Kathy for an update. Minutes later, her phone buzzed once more.

"Is this Kathy?"

"Yes, it is."

"Okay." It was a man's voice, not young sounding. He paused and took a deep breath. "My name is Ned Pierce. I saw the picture of your missing person in *The Beacon*. That's our local newspaper here in Bakersfield, California."

"Thanks for calling, Mr. Pierce. Have you ever seen Mr. Hutchinson?" Kathy asked.

"Well, the thing is, I'm pretty sure I darn near ran that guy over back in 1970."

Kathy was wary: 1970 seemed like a *long* time ago. "How do you know we're talking about the same man, Mr. Pierce?"

"I don't, not for sure, anyway. But I'd bet on it, even though I had no idea who he was back then," he replied. "It was early in the morning, an hour before sunrise. We were in the middle of nowhere."

"Where was that?" Kathy asked.

"Just before you get to Skull Valley, Arizona, on the county road," the man replied. "I can't remember the highway name."

Now he had Kathy's full attention. She put the call on speaker and raced over to Pete, whose head was stuck in the refrigerator. "County road 10," Kathy replied. "What were you doing out there?"

"Driving a truck from Prescott to Barstow, California, a six-hour trip with some stops in rural areas along the way. Someone stumbled out onto the road right in front of my truck. I hammered my brakes and swerved, but you can't stop a semi on a dime. After I pulled over, I ran back and found him in the ditch."

The siblings grimaced, fearing the worst.

Mr. Pierce continued. "To this day, I don't understand how I missed him. First thing I noticed—his clothes were damp. The poor guy was freezing, shaking and shivering like a dog. I never picked up hitchhikers—company rules. But the boy wasn't hitching. I figured he had hurt himself, but he didn't appear to be hurt, not physically, anyway. Still, *something* was wrong—no way could I leave him out there. It was dark as the ace of spades and I was fearful he'd get run over. 'Get in,' I told him. And he did."

"So you got a good look at him?" Kathy asked.

"Oh, yeah. He crawled up into the cabin—I turned the heat on full blast to warm the kid up. He stunk to high heaven—must have been that pond mentioned in the *Beacon*. I spent the next seven hours with him. He was the spitting image of the boy in that yearbook photo you published—no way could you miss him. I figured he was sixteen—not much younger than I was on my first job."

"Sir, my brother Pete has a question."

"Go ahead."

"Did he identify himself?"

"That was the thing," the older man replied. "I wondered what he was doing out there in the middle of nowhere, and he couldn't answer. Then I asked him his name—he said he didn't know. So I called him Sam. That was my boss's name."

"What happened next?" Kathy asked. She held her breath.

"I told him my last stop was Barstow. 'Fine with me,' he said. So away we went. The kid didn't have a dime on him. I bought him a big breakfast at a diner an hour and a half down the road. Man, he was hungry, that's for sure. When we got to Barstow, I gave him a few bucks and let him off on Interstate 40. Never saw him again."

"What did he talk about, Mr. Pierce?" Pete asked. "Can you remember anything he told you?"

"Oh, sure, that's easy. He never talked about anything. Didn't know his own name, not even his age. Nor where he hailed from. Plus, except for breakfast, he slept most of the way. There was one thing, though."

"What's that?" Pete asked.

"Well, I figured he was ill—anyone who's forgotten his name has a problem, right? I offered to drop him off at a hospital, or a police station, but he didn't like that. So it occurred to me that he might even be a fugitive, but he seemed awful young to be on the run. When I read the report in this morning's newspaper, it all made sense. That boy had been in a serious accident."

The call ended minutes later with the Brunellis thanking Mr. Pierce. The siblings looked at each other, barely containing their excitement.

"He survived." Kathy cried. *"He survived!"*

14

MARIA

S uzanne was beside herself. "After you called, we didn't know what to do with ourselves, we were so excited."

"Mom thought we had lost it," Tom said, grinning.

The Brunellis had raced over to the Jacksons' to discuss the blockbuster news.

"That call was a heck of a break," Pete said. "Now we're *sure* that Grant survived, he didn't drown. Somehow, he got out of there. Had to be that open window on the driver's side."

"Without a clue who he was," Suzanne noted. "He must have slammed his head a good one to cause such severe amnesia."

"We checked it out online," Kathy said. "There's something called 'severe retrograde amnesia.' It's often caused by traumatic brain injury—emotional trauma can play a role too—and in rare cases individuals may completely forget who they are."

"Oh, wow," Suzanne said. "So the poor guy still suffers from it. Otherwise, he would have contacted his family. No wonder they never heard from him."

Tom's mind spun. "After he escaped from the pond, he walked north, all the way to the county highway."

"Before riding west to California," Pete said. "There's a good chance that's where he lives today."

"The odd thing," Kathy said, "is that whoever created the treasure map must have survived the accident too. And that person walked *south*, I'd bet anything."

"I'll tell you what," Suzanne said, "the mystery lady believed Grant never made it out of there, did she?"

"That's the truth," Tom said. "How weird is that?"

Pete couldn't wrap his arms around the secondary mystery—or was it the third? "How come she never mentioned the other girl—the one in the car? Not a word in the treasure map."

"She did," Kathy argued.

"How?"

"The title on the map is 'My Treasure Map.' You can read 'treasure' as singular or plural. The two people in that car *were* her treasure."

Suzanne said, "Whoa, Kathy, I think you're right."

Tom said, "Well, we all agree there's a good possibility Grant Dorrance Hutchinson is alive today—and living under a different identity."

"The man who doesn't know who he is," Kathy said, her eyes shining. "But I'm willing to bet his first name is Sam."

Just then, the sheriff called. The foursome quickly filled him in.

"Well, that's quite a revelation, isn't it?" he responded. "It stuck with that guy all those years. Now I've got something for you. The DNA report came in—no matches to the skeleton. The only thing it tells us is the young lady's heritage points toward Northern Europe."

"That's it?" Tom asked, disappointed.

"Nope. The reward for finding Mr. Dorrance expired in 1995."

"Darn it," Pete muttered.

THE GIRLS HEADED OUT TO CALL ON MISS HUTCHINSON. THEY

couldn't wait to deliver the astonishing news. Meanwhile, the boys were in the archival center of *The Daily Pilot*, searching through obituaries.

Pete asked, "What are our search parameters?"

"An older female, nothing more. A woman died, but there's no clue who, when, or where," Tom conceded. "We'll read the profiles of each obituary and see if something jumps out at us."

"It's a long shot," Pete said, "searching back weeks or months too."

"Worse. Try years."

"Geez. Start at the top and work down."

It was a grueling search. They clicked on one obituary after another and glanced through a few lines of each. Turned out a couple dozen Prescott area people died every month—and not a few of them had led remarkable lives.

"Keep reading their life stories and we'll be here all night," Pete groused.

Nothing seemed to connect with the case.

"Nope, she wasn't even here in 'seventy . . .This one moved here five years ago . . . Charlotte was a teacher in Ash Fork, not likely . . . Too young . . . Too old . . . Peggy was in a medical facility, with a rare disease. . . Lisa was overseas . . . She came from Arkansas . . . Canada . . . England . . . Lithuania."

"Lithuania?" Pete repeated. "Who comes from there?"

"Lithuanians."

The hunt dragged on. From the week before the drop-off at St. Vincent de Paul, they moved to the previous month. Then three months. Six months. One year. Nothing.

"Maybe she didn't die in Prescott," Tom said.

"In which case, this is hopeless," a dispirited Pete replied.

But they kept going, until—

"Hey, Pete, here's an interesting one."

"Whataya got?"

"Maria Louisa Rodriquez, in her seventies, died at Prescott Regional Hospital, September last year. Check out her photo."

The obituary photograph, obviously taken at a much younger age, showed an uncommonly beautiful young lady with long black hair. She had high cheekbones, attractive oval eyes, and a luminous smile. Very fetching.

Pete whistled. "Wow. What a beauty." He laughed. "Is that why she's interesting?"

"Well, you have to admit . . ." Tom said with a chuckle. "No, seriously, listen to this." One line of her obituary notice stood out: "'Maria spent her life working as a maid for a handful of Prescott's leading families.'"

"Oh, boy, you might have something here," Pete said. "I wonder if Miss Hutchinson knew her."

"I'll message Suzanne," Tom said, pulling out his cell phone.

MEANWHILE, MISS DAISY HUTCHINSON WAS ALMOST SPEECHLESS.

"Do—do you believe Mr. Pierce?" she stammered.

"Yes," Kathy said. "The call came to me. My brother, Pete, and I talked to him for quite some time. It all made sense."

"And it sure explains why Grant wasn't in the car."

"Or the pond," Kathy said.

Miss Hutchinson rose and walked over to the large picture window. She heaved a deep sigh, twisting her arms in front of her. It was obvious she was trying to gain control of her emotions.

"All these years—wasted. Didn't police departments even bother talking to one another back then?" She sighed again before turning around to face them. "Now what?"

"Now we wait for the next lead," Kathy said.

"We've been getting a few calls every day," Suzanne explained. "Except for Mr. Pierce, they've all been nuisance calls. But it appears as if your brother was last seen in Barstow."

Kathy said, "Yes. We're hopeful."

Suzanne received a text message from Tom.

"Here's a question from my brother," she said, reading from the screen and addressing Miss Hutchinson. "Are you familiar with someone named Maria Louisa Rodriquez?"

"Oh, surely." She returned to her seat and sat down. "Maria was a favorite maid in my parents' household when I was in eighth grade. She was four years older than me. Everyone loved her. I hadn't seen Maria in years. She died last year—I read her obituary in the newspaper. Very sad."

"How long did she work for you?"

"I'm only guessing when I say two years. Why is your brother asking?"

"I'm not sure." Suzanne texted the answers to Tom. He replied: *When did she leave the Hutchinsons?*

"He's asking when she left her job," Suzanne said.

"Just days after Grant disappeared," she replied. Her eyes became distant. "Maria couldn't handle the drama. My father had become quite unhinged. He had a terrible temper and blamed everyone but himself. But *he* was the one who bought Grant that hot car against my mother's wishes. Maria couldn't deal with the situation—the whole thing was too emotional for her. She quit."

Just then, Suzanne's cell phone buzzed.

15

THE ROAD WEST

"Hey, your post pulled up a lead," Sheriff McClennan said. "I'm going to text you a name and phone number. The man's name is Hal Turner, and he's a former officer with the California Highway Patrol. Call him—he's got an interesting story."

"Will do, sir." Suzanne said. She disconnected. "The sheriff has a lead for us, Miss Hutchinson. Would you like to be on this call?"

"Yes, I would."

Suzanne tapped the highlighted number in the text from the sheriff and set her phone on speaker. Seconds later, Mr. Turner answered.

"Mr. Turner," she began, "my name is Suzanne Jackson. Sheriff McClennan asked us to reach out to you. You're on speaker with my friend Kathy Brunelli and Miss Daisy Hutchinson."

"Yes, hello. I've been expecting your call."

"You have something for us?"

"I do. Someone shared your post on a highway patrol page. Let me tell you, that young man wouldn't be easy to forget. He was a good-looking kid, well-spoken, with impeccable manners. But he carried no identification. For an officer, that's a red flag."

"You picked him up?" Kathy asked. "Where?"

"Yeah, back in 1970, and I've never forgotten him. I was a rookie California Highway Patrol officer, assigned to Bakersfield. As the new guy on board, I worked the late shift. One night I spotted a young man hitchhiking on Highway 99, just south of the city—after midnight. That's an unusual time to hitchhike, which is the reason I stopped him. But he had no ID, no money. Nothing."

"Isn't it illegal not to carry identification?" Suzanne asked.

"Not in California," he replied. "Some states have 'stop and iden- tify' statutes that require someone to provide identification to police, making refusal to do so a crime. California has no such statute—there's no arrest if you refuse a request for ID while police are detaining you."

"So having no ID made him memorable?" Kathy asked.

"No, that happened every so often. What *was* unusual is that he only provided a first name. No last name or hometown. And no clue where he was going. He tried hard to provide answers. I could tell he wasn't being evasive—*he just didn't know*. I figured he was sick and offered to drive him to the county hospital, but he refused. Nice kid, but something was wrong—I couldn't put my finger on it, but there were no grounds to hold him. So I gave him five bucks, wished him luck, and let him go. But he's your guy, without a shred of doubt. When I saw your post online, I remembered that face as if it were yesterday."

Miss Hutchinson spoke up. "Mr. Turner, you mentioned a first name."

"I'm not positive now," the ex-officer replied, "but 'Sam' comes to mind. There was no *last* name. In my twenty-five years of being a CHP officer, I never had another one like that."

"Did he mention where he was going?" Suzanne asked.

"Yup: he said he was on the way to Nowhere."

"*'Nowhere'?*"

"Uh-huh. It's a ghost town in Arizona. I figured he must have passed through it the night before. It must have popped into his mind when I asked—he was trying real hard to find answers to my questions. 'I'm going to Nowhere,' he said. 'You're heading in the wrong direction,' I told him. He got out of my car and walked south on 99—to a different 'nowhere,' I guess. An hour passed before I circled back. Someone had picked him up. After reading your post, I felt bad. But there wasn't much I could do for the young fellow."

"Don't feel bad, Mr. Turner," Miss Hutchinson replied. Her voice caught. "I thank you for helping my brother."

LATER, THE FOURSOME MET AT THE SHAKE SHOP TO COMPARE NOTES. They sat out on a picnic table and ordered iced teas.

"We had great timing," Kathy explained, her eyes sparkling. "So out of the blue we get this ex–California Highway Patrol officer on the phone, right there with Miss Hutchinson, and he tells us he picked Grant up outside Bakersfield." She told the story, almost without stopping to breathe.

"For the first time since his disappearance, Miss Hutchinson is crossing her fingers, hoping her brother survived whatever happened that day," Suzanne said. "He might even be alive now. And his new name was Sam, a gift from Ned Pierce, the truck driver, don't you think?"

"To sum up:" Kathy said, "he caught a ride outside Skull Valley to Barstow, and then hitchhiked to Bakersfield. The last sighting was Grant hitching on highway 99, south of the city."

"This is amazing," Tom exclaimed. "Your post worked so well that we're tracking this guy's movement half a century later. *Great* idea, Kathy."

She grinned.

"Where does highway 99 go?" Pete asked.

Suzanne brought up Google Maps on her cell phone. "It runs into Interstate 5 and continues to Los Angeles, almost a straight line south."

The iced teas arrived, and Kathy passed them around. "Sugar, anyone?" She avoided the stuff like the plague.

Suzanne said, "Bet anything that's where he still lives today."

"*If* he's alive."

"Expect more calls," Pete said.

"I've got an idea," Kathy said. "Let's repost tonight. See if we can reach more online social networks. I'll add on a line about Grant possibly going by 'Sam' and perhaps living in the Los Angeles area."

"Super thought, Kathy," Tom exclaimed. "By reposting, we'll stir up more action."

"Now . . . about Maria Louisa Rodriquez," Suzanne said.

"And the shooter," Kathy prompted.

"I have a hunch Maria is our mystery woman," Tom said. "It's way too much of a coincidence that she was working for the Hutchinson family when Grant disappeared. I'm betting she's the one who drew the treasure map."

"And escaped the pond when the car went in," Pete added. "But what does it all mean?"

"Well," Suzanne said, "It points to a—"

"Romantic interest," Kathy said firmly. "Between a maid and her employer's son. Very inappropriate, to say the least. Lord, no wonder she quit. I can't imagine her inner emotional turmoil. Apparently, no one in the Hutchinson family had a clue."

"Still doesn't," Suzanne figured. She recalled Miss Hutchinson's words: *"My father had become unhinged. He had a terrible temper and blamed everyone but himself."* That was one detail she and Kathy hadn't mentioned. "Miss Hutchinson made it clear that her father could be frightening. If Adolph Hutchinson had known about Grant and Maria . . ."

No need to finish the sentence.

"Any thoughts on the other girl?" Pete asked. "The one in the Dodge? Who was she?"

Silence.

"Okay," Suzanne said, locking eyes with her brother. "So you think the guy who dropped the books off at the thrift store is the shooter. Why?"

"Well, it's nothing more than a strong hunch," Tom replied. "But whoever dropped off those books is hiding something."

"That would explain the unusual night-time drop," Pete said. "No way did he want his identity revealed."

"You know what's weird? Tom asked. "Why bother? I mean, why not just throw the books in the garbage can?"

Suzanne, the book lover, understood. "The mystery woman asked him to donate them—that's why. And he agreed."

"Ah-ha," Kathy said. "Sure. But he didn't want to connect the books to her, dead or not. He *knew* about Skull Valley and the Super Bee."

"You must be right, Tom!" Suzanne exclaimed. "Because he found his way out to the pond. Even the newspaper didn't publish the directions."

"But he *couldn't* have known about the treasure map," Tom said. "Otherwise, those books would all have been trashed."

Pete said, "His goal was to protect the mystery woman, even in death."

"There's more to this story," Tom said. He shook his head. "There has to be. He's protecting himself too. I mean, think about it. He shot at us, trying to scare us away from the case. That's radical, isn't it?"

"You bet it is," Suzanne said. "Too radical just to protect a dead woman's reputation. Dangerous and criminal too. There's something else going on."

"Must have been a nasty surprise when he read the story in *The Daily Pilot*," Kathy said. "Okay, what now?"

"Well, we have to trace the distant footsteps of Maria Louisa Rodriquez," Pete said. "Her obituary stated that she died last year, but where did she live? Who did she associate with? Where did she work? What do they know about her?"

"If she *is* the one who penned the treasure map," Tom said, "she'll lead us straight back to the shooter."

Suzanne eyed him gravely. "Don't tell Mom."

———————

THAT EVENING THE TWINS AND THE BRUNELLI SIBLINGS ALL JUMPED online. Each of them released the new post on their favorite social media sites, highlighting 'Sam' and Los Angeles as possibilities.

"Now we wait," Kathy said. After the call with Mr. Turner, her cell phone had gone silent.

Typing 'Maria Louisa Rodriquez + Prescott, AZ' into a search engine, they scoured the Web. It didn't take long.

"Look at this," Suzanne said. "Her Facebook page is still up."

"So there is life after death," Kathy quipped.

"Happens all the time," Pete said. "It is a little macabre."

Maria materialized before their eyes. Her Facebook images showed a slightly overweight Hispanic woman, seventy-plus, with long, gray-streaked hair and a smiling face. She had a hundred and twenty friends online and had uploaded dozens of pictures.

There had been no men in her life. Just an active, older lady—she had loved to hike—with a longish list of friends who had lots of children.

Before long, Tom found her last address. A few years earlier, Maria had moved to a small house—"The first home I've ever purchased!"—in the city's poorer area, and proudly published the address in her newsfeed. A younger, more internet-savvy person would not have done that, they all knew.

And it was Suzanne who spotted a caption below a photo: House Manager for the Brandenburg Family. *"Bingo!"* she cried.

16

CHASING LEADS

K athy's phone buzzed again early on Thursday, right after breakfast. She answered with a cheerful, "Good morning!"

"Hello," a young woman replied. "My name is Elinore Russell, and I saw your post online. I recognize that man."

"Thank you for calling, Elinore. Where did you see him?"

"I own a coffee shop in Thousand Oaks, California. Sam came in here every morning until a year ago."

Kathy felt her heart begin to beat faster. "Is that a suburb of Los Angeles?"

"Yes, it is."

"You *sure* your customer Sam is the same man as in the forensic artist's drawings?"

"No doubt at all," Elinor replied. "I talked to him often. And he's the spitting image of the pictures you posted online—the older ones, I mean. Except he had more hair."

Kathy was almost afraid to ask the question. "What happened a year ago?"

"He told me he and his wife had sold their home to move closer to the beach. He came in for one last cup of coffee and to say good-bye. Very nice man."

Kathy let out a sigh of relief. "Any idea of his surname, or where he worked?"

"Sorry. I don't."

"What about his wife's name?"

"Nope, I never met her."

Kathy thanked Elinore, disconnected, then raced downstairs to tell Pete. "Closer!" she said. "We're zeroing in."

THE BRANDENBURGS WERE EASY TO FIND. JULIA BRANDENBURG HAD been in the twins' seventh- and eighth-grade classes at St. Francis Elementary School. The family lived a few blocks away.

Julia, a big girl with a personality to match, gave each of the twins a hug on the front porch. "I read about that car you found by Skull Valley. Wow! What's going on?"

"We're wondering what you can tell us about Maria Louisa Rodriquez," Suzanne said.

"Maria? Was she involved in that?"

Tom said, "We're not positive. Not yet, anyway."

"Well, our family loved Maria, that's for sure," Julia said. "Our hearts broke when she died."

Julia's mother joined them. "Tom and Suzanne, how *are* you?" More hugs.

"We're doing great, Mrs. Brandenburg," the twins chorused.

"Mom, they're asking about Maria."

"Maria? Oh, my goodness," Mrs. Brandenburg said. "We still miss her. Why are you asking?"

No way did the twins want to reveal their suspicions about Maria and Grant and their possible connection to the sunken car. Not yet, anyway.

After a moment's hesitation, Suzanne broke the ice. "Well, there was a connection between Maria and the Hutchinson family. We're trying to figure it out."

"Oh, that's easy," Julia's mother replied. "She worked for them as a maid—her first job."

"Any idea why Maria left the Hutchinsons?" Tom asked.

"Well," Mrs. Brandenburg replied, "we understood that Adolph Hutchinson was a tyrant with a mean streak. In the days after Grant disappeared, he went on a rampage that terrified Maria. He frightened her half to death."

"You couldn't find a more wonderful person," Julia said. "She ran our household since as far back as I remember."

"Almost twenty years," Mrs. Brandenburg said, nodded approvingly. "We thought of her as part of the family."

"Never married?" Tom asked.

"Never."

"Did she have a boyfriend?"

"No," Julia said firmly. "We always wondered why. She was such a beautiful person, inside and out."

"And no living relatives, right?" Suzanne asked.

"Correct. Right, Mom?"

"Well, there was one."

Julia's eyes widened. "Really? I didn't know. She never talked about her family."

"For good reason," Mrs. Brandenburg said, pursing her lips. "Her parents died young, but she had a brother who went bad. Maria only mentioned him once, right after she joined our family."

That revelation surprised Tom. There was no mention of a survivor in Maria's brief obituary. "When you say 'bad,' Mrs. Brandenburg . . ."

"Well, she never told me. Whatever he did, it was bad enough that it caused her to break off all relations with him. She said she wouldn't ever talk to him again."

Tom held his breath. "Did she mention his name?"

There was a pause while everyone looked at Mrs. Brandenburg expectantly. "Yes, she mentioned it, but that was so long ago. It—it was an unusual name, that I do recall. But for the life of me, I can't remember what it was."

Meanwhile, Pete and Kathy were busy pouring over missing-persons reports, searching for the identity of the young lady in the car. They searched a time frame extending from one week before to three months after Grant's disappearance.

The Chief had made the city police records available to them, but they found nothing but endless files on Grant himself. "The sheriff's investigators were already here a few days ago," the Chief confessed. "They spent hours going through the same material but came up empty."

So did the Brunellis. They called Heidi and drove a few blocks over to *The Daily Pilot.*

Heidi ushered the siblings into the paper's archives, where they searched for another two hours using the same time parameters. No other reports appeared of missing persons in Prescott or the surrounding area.

A little later, the twins met their friends outside the *Pilot's* offices to catch up with them with their big news.

"We think he's Maria's brother," Suzanne said.

Kathy looked at her. "You mean the guy who dropped the books off?"

"Yup. Mrs. Brandenburg said that Maria had mentioned him, but only once. He was a bad one, she said—always getting into trouble. Maria cut him off."

"Okay," Pete said. "But now that raises the question, if Maria cut her brother off, how did he get hold of her books after she died?"

"Good question," Kathy said. "Now what?"

"Now we go say 'hello,'" Tom said.

17

A CLOSE CALL

"What do you mean?" Suzanne asked, locking eyes with her brother. "How do we know where this guy is?"

"I don't," Tom replied. "At least, not for sure. But if he has access to her personal belongings—"

"Such as her beloved books, for example—" Kathy said.

Pete got it. "So you're thinking he's living in her house."

"It's possible," Tom said. "There's one way to find out."

"Okay," Suzanne said. "So we like, uh, just go knock on his door?"

"Sure, why not? We'll know right off the bat whether it's the same guy we spotted on the security footage—or not."

———

In Arizona, the midsummer sun sets around seven forty in the evening. The mystery searchers slipped into place minutes before, trying to look inconspicuous where they sat parked in the twilight, one door away from what had been Maria's home. Their position afforded them an angled view of the smallish house, built on a narrow lot on Sixth Street in one of the older parts of the city. The property had seen better days: a picket fence with its gate swinging open bordered the sidewalk, protecting a patch of sorry-looking grass that needed watering. A sagging two-step porch led to the front door. The dilapidation stood apart from Maria's pride when she had first bought the house and posted on Facebook.

In the unpaved driveway on one side of the house sat a dark-colored, old-model four-door sedan.

"Like the one on the security video," Pete said. "It's a common vehicle though."

His sister rolled her eyes. "We've heard that before."

Someone was home.

Moments after sunset, a light clicked on, glowing through yellow kitchen curtains on the house's west side. Pete stepped out of the Chevy for a survey, but the light cut off seconds later. Just then, the front windows—the living room, they figured—lit up. A man walked up to the picture window, his gaze averted, and pulled the curtains closed.

Tom groaned. "We missed our chance."

Pete jumped back into the car. "What now?"

"Didn't see a thing," Suzanne said.

"Well, let's ring his doorbell," Pete suggested. He was serious too.

"Oh, sure," his sister replied. "Then what?"

"Then we ask him about Maria," Tom said. "It's all aboveboard. He can tell us any lie he wants, but we'll get a good look at him. Why not? That's our goal."

Pete said. "Who's coming with me?"

"I am," Kathy answered, already halfway out the car. She didn't want her brother to earn all the glory.

"Go for it," Suzanne said. She pulled her cell phone from her purse, tapped the center of the frame to improve the exposure, and zoomed in towards the front door. "I'll capture video of the scene."

"And I'll be your backup," Tom said to the Brunellis.

The siblings hustled through the gate—it squealed as Kathy pushed it open—and onto the porch. Tom stayed behind them, on the lawn below, off to one side. Pete looked for a doorbell without success. He knocked on the outside screen door. The inside front door was wide open.

An impatient male voice shouted, "Whataya want?"

Pete shouted back. "We have a question—about Maria!"

A tall, slender man appeared at the screen door. They could barely see him, silhouetted in the dark hallway. He turned on an outside porch light, lighting up the threesome—and himself: an angry face, jeans and a white t-shirt.

"What about her?" he snarled.

He recognizes us, Kathy realized with a start. "Are you her brother?" she asked.

In an instant, the man turned ugly. "Get off my doorstep!" he bellowed.

"Were you the one who dropped the books off?" Pete asked in a measured voice.

"Get off my property!" the man demanded.

"Were they yours or Maria's?"

That did it. The man hammered the screen door open. Unexpectedly, he had one hand wrapped around a baseball bat, which rose in a wild swing. Kathy ducked and lost her balance, falling backward off the porch onto the front yard. Pete reached back instinctively to grab his sister's hand, but the man hadn't finished. He reared back and swung again, smashing Pete's left arm just below the shoulder.

Pete screamed in pain just as Tom leaped onto the steps and dived straight into the unhinged man, who hollered as he fell backward into the house. He scrambled to his feet, then slammed the front door in Tom's face—and locked it.

Suzanne had caught the action on video. With her phone camera still rolling, she tapped 911 and rushed to help Kathy to her feet. Tom wrapped his arm around Pete—doubled over in agony—and the four hustled back to their car.

A long minute passed before a siren shrieked in the distance.

"THIS GUY HAS A RECORD LONGER THAN MY ARM," SAID THE CHIEF, leaning back in his chair.

It was the morning after the brouhaha. Tom had called the Chief, asking for a meeting at police headquarters. As the four friends trooped in, the Chief chatted with Sheriff McClennan on speaker while reviewing the digital file on Chester "Chuck" Rodriquez. The revealing document had arrived in both men's email inboxes a while earlier from Arizona State Prison.

The previous evening, as the four young sleuths watched, and relying on their eyewitness testimony and video evidence, the police had arrested "Bob Smith"—as he called himself—for aggravated assault and battery with a deadly weapon. After a routine fingerprint check, they identified the suspect as Rodriquez—Maria's brother.

"Say, how's the arm, Pete?" the Chief asked. "That's one heck of a bruise."

"No sweat," Pete replied, feeling gently around the sensitive area. "Luckily, he caught me right on the muscle. Otherwise he'd have broken the bone for sure."

"How'd you get onto this guy?" the sheriff asked.

"The Brandenburg family," Suzanne explained. "Maria had been their housekeeper for years. In all that time, she had mentioned her brother's name only once, and said he had gone bad. Mrs. Brandenburg couldn't remember it, but—"

"We suspected that Maria must have been the author of the treasure map," Kathy cut in, "and that her brother might have been the one who dropped off the books."

"And that he was living in her home," Tom said.

"Turns out," Pete said, "we were right."

"Good, solid detective work," the Chief said. "Rodriquez has spent more time in prison than out," he added with a snort. "Man, he's a mean one."

"You still got him locked up?" the sheriff asked.

"Yeah, but his court-appointed attorney says he'll make bail later today."

"They should have kept him in the state pen for another twenty years," the sheriff groused.

"What crimes did he commit?" Tom asked.

The Chief paused for a few seconds as he scanned his computer screen. "Breaking and entering, burglary, car theft, carrying a stolen concealed weapon, assault with a deadly weapon—this guy is no Boy Scout. His most recent conviction was for armed robbery in Phoenix. That earned him a nice, long stretch in the state pen."

"When was he released?" Pete asked.

"September first, last year."

"There you go," Kathy said, adding it up. "Maria died later that same month."

"Okay," Tom said. "So that's when he reconnected with her. That explains how he gained possession of her books."

"And everything else she owned, it looks like," Suzanne said.

"Including her house," Pete said.

Sheriff McClennan's voice boomed over the speakerphone. "Looks as if he's been operating out of Phoenix for decades."

"Yeah, I noticed that too," the Chief said. "But his first burglary conviction occurred in Prescott in 1969. He went to prison for a year."

"Released in 1970," the sheriff continued. "Next thing we know, he's arrested in Phoenix in November 1971 and charged with burglary—his second offense. Looks as if he picked up some bad habits while he was in prison."

"Every other charge is from Phoenix," the Chief said. "And there are quite a few of them—including that assault with a deadly weapon. That's a bad one, and then he raised the ante."

"He sure did," the sheriff said. "Armed robbery. That sent him behind bars for a stretch."

"Seven to ten," the Chief said, "and they kept him locked up for eight. It says here he assaulted a guy in prison too—warns against his mean temper."

"We can attest to that," Kathy quipped.

The sheriff coughed once. "A real solid citizen. What's he up to now?"

"Other than shooting at us and trying to break Pete's arm," Suzanne said, "it appears as if he's been handling Maria's affairs."

"That's what we wanted to talk about," Tom said. "We need to locate two items that would help cement this case."

The Chief tapped his fingers on the desk. "Such as?"

"The rifle he used at us in the desert," Kathy said. "Where is it?"

"And," Suzanne said, "it would be very nice if we could locate a sample of Maria's handwriting. That would confirm our suspicions—"

"That she's the mystery writer of the treasure map," Pete said.

The Chief beamed. "Okay, I'm all in on both counts. What do you think, Sheriff?"

"Yeah, let's go for it," the sheriff's voice boomed over the speaker. "But we better move fast. I'll get a search warrant today. Let's meet out at Maria's house later this afternoon. Who knows? We might get lucky."

THE TWO OFFICERS PULLED UP FIRST, FOLLOWED BY THE MUSTANG with the four young sleuths. They all stepped out to the curb of Maria's home where they found a team of evidence technicians already at work. Two techs were searching the Ford sedan parked on the gravel driveway.

"Now that we're seeing it by daylight," Pete said, "I feel even more sure that's the car we saw at the loading dock in the security footage."

"Agreed," Tom said.

A rifle, wrapped up with rags, appeared in the trunk: a .30-.30 Winchester—a match for the bullets that deputies had found in the desert. Huge grins appeared on the senior officers' faces. They high-fived each other.

"Pretty weird for old guys," Kathy whispered with a wry expression on her face.

Minutes later, a tech handed the Chief an 8x11 notebook. "I found it in a kitchen drawer," he said. "It's like a daily to-do list, and it has Maria's name on the inside cover."

"Well," said the Chief, passing it over to the foursome, "what do you think? Do you recognize the style of her writing?"

The mystery searchers gathered around at stared at the familiar cursive script before glancing at one another.

"Identical," Tom said.

"There you go," Suzanne said. "I'm certain your forensic handwriting experts will confirm that."

"And without doubt her brother wrote that note inviting us for a walk in the desert," Pete said. He frowned at the memory.

The Chief grinned. "We'll run a check on the signature he provided when we booked him in, but in my mind there's little doubt."

18

A FELLOW NAMED SAM

E arly on Friday morning—now two weeks after the mystery searchers had started on the case—Kathy's cell phone rang.

"Is this Kathy?" It was a woman, an elderly lady, to judge by her voice.

"Yes, it is."

"I spotted your post last evening. You're looking for Sam Fellow."

"I'm sorry," Kathy replied. "I didn't catch your name."

"Marlene. The pictures you posted are of Sam Fellow."

"Do you know him, Marlene?"

"Not well, but he lived down the street from me in Thousand Oaks. He and his wife moved out about a year ago."

By then, Kathy was racing around the house, her cell phone on speaker, looking for Pete.

"And he looks like the drawings we posted?"

"The clean shaven one. Identical. Except he has more hair."

"Any idea of his wife's name?"

"Claudia."

Kathy wanted to do a handstand for joy. Instead, she settled for a high-five from her brother.

"Any clue where they moved to?"

"No, but I'll ask the neighbors. Can I call you back?"

An hour later, the twins arrived at the Brunellis', laptops in hand. All four friends settled in the living room, searching online for Sam Fellow.

"An unusual name," Suzanne said.

"Well, think about it," Tom replied. "'A fellow named Sam.' It makes perfect sense. The man with no memory of his identity except the first name Sam, provided by a stranger. He just made it up."

Kathy's cell phone rang again.

"Hi, Marlene. What did you find out?"

"Ventura. They moved to Ventura, California."

"Wonderful, thank you so much."

"You're most welcome," Marlene said. "I sure hope you find him. He's an awfully nice guy."

"We'll let you know."

Suzanne tried information in Ventura. No listing.

"Doesn't appear to have a landline," Pete said. The four continued their search, focusing on Ventura.

Two nuisance calls rolled in, including a reporter from San Francisco with lots of questions. "Under advice from our local police, we cannot comment on an ongoing investigation," Kathy said.

"Gimme something, anything?" the reporter pleaded.

"There is nothing firm," Kathy replied. "When there is, I'll call you back. Okay?" That would have to do.

It wasn't thirty minutes later that Kathy's cell phone rang again. "Wow, I'm sure popular today. Hi, this is Kathy." She put the call on speaker.

There was a pause before they heard a woman's voice. "I think you're looking for my father."

The four looked at one another, holding their collective breath. *Could it be?*

Kathy asked, "May I ask your name?"

"Meryl Miller."

Suzanne jumped to her feet. "Did she say *'Meryl'*?" she hissed.

"Did you say 'Meryl'?" Kathy asked.

"Yes. My married name is Miller. My maiden name is Fellow."

"How do you spell your first name?"

"M-E-R-Y-L."

By now, all four of the mystery searchers were on their feet. Pete couldn't stand still—he paced the living room in circles.

"Where do you live, Meryl?"

"Thousand Oaks, but my parents live in Ventura."

"So I assume you saw our missing-person post?"

"Yes. That's my father, for sure. For the first time, we saw where he came from. Does he have family in Prescott?"

"He surely does," Kathy replied. "A wonderful sister named Daisy. You're on speaker with other people who have been searching for your father."

"Meryl, my name is Tom Jackson. It's our belief your dad survived an accident in which he escaped from a submerged car near Skull Valley, Arizona. Has he ever mentioned anything about it?"

"I read that in your post," Meryl said, "but he knows nothing about that. His first memory is walking across a desert trail, almost freezing to death, and reaching a highway. A trucker stopped and picked him up. He often says his life began that day."

Joyous eyes flashed around the room.

"Hi, Meryl, my name is Suzanne Jackson. I have to tell you something that may astonish you."

"Go ahead."

"Your grandmother's first name was Meryl."

Meryl sounded choked up, but when Suzanne gently suggested a follow-up phone call the following day from Ventura . . . with Sam Fellow . . . and Miss Daisy Hutchinson—she agreed.

IT WAS TIME FOR ANOTHER MEETING WITH THE ELEGANT LADY.

"You guys come with us too," Suzanne said to the boys. "She trusts us now, and I'm sure she'll welcome you."

Sarah, though surprised to see the four friends when she opened the door, didn't show a moment's hesitation. The two girls introduced their brothers.

"Very pleased to meet you," Sarah said, "and Miss Hutchinson will be too. Please come in and make yourselves comfortable. I'll fetch tea"—she stopped and glanced back at them—"or would you all prefer coffee?"

"Coffee all around, Sarah, thank you," Pete replied.

Two minutes later, Miss Hutchinson stepped into the room, a smile crossing her face. Introductions followed.

"We're very pleased to meet you," Tom said as they shook hands. So much had happened, and so quickly. The boys felt as if they already knew Grant's sister.

"Likewise," she replied. "Please make yourselves comfortable."

"Miss Hutchinson, we have a lot to talk about," Suzanne said.

"And we have good news to share with you," Kathy said. She looked at her best friend. "Go ahead, Suzie. This all started with you."

"We believe we've found your brother. He calls himself Sam Fellow, and he'll be calling you tomorrow morning at ten."

Miss Hutchinson passed out cold.

19

A CRIME FROM THE PAST

The twins caught the older woman as her legs buckled, preventing a nasty spill on the hard wooden floor. Kathy screamed out, *"Sarah!"* as the four helped to settle Miss Hutchinson in a favorite chair.

The ever-immaculate maid brought in a cold cloth and pressed it to her forehead.

"I'm so sorry," Miss Hutchinson said, after her head cleared. "That wasn't very polite of me."

The girls had never seen her like this before. She was on pins and needles, animated and tense at the same time.

"We understand," Pete said. "It must have been quite a shock."

"Well, my hopes were up, but it didn't seem possible—Grant disappeared half a century ago. Tell me, please, what makes you so positive you've found my brother."

The girls handled most of the ensuing discussion. "He remembers being picked up by a trucker in Arizona . . . his cloths were wet . . . the officer remembered him . . . he has often called it the day his life began."

Near the end of the story, Suzanne got to the part where the caller—Grant's daughter—turned out to be named Meryl.

Miss Hutchinson's eye brimmed with tears. Sarah brought tissues. "That is so strange. If he didn't know his own identity, where would he find the name Meryl?"

"The human mind is complex, isn't it?" Suzanne said.

"It surely is. His wife's name is . . ."

"Claudia."

"Any other children?"

"We didn't ask."

Later, after Miss Hutchinson had settled down, Kathy spoke up. "We have something else to tell you, and it will be a quite a shock."

She visibly steeled herself. "All right. I'm ready."

"We discovered the identity of the mystery writer—the person who wrote that letter to you in 1981 and penned the treasure map."

Apprehension seemed to flood the lady. "Well?"

"Maria Louisa Rodriquez."

A stunned silence ensued before she cried out, "Wait! *What?*" Then, "I don't believe it!"

"It's true," Suzanne said. "The sheriff arrested her brother a few hours ago. He had moved into her home."

"Impossible," Miss Hutchinson said, folding her arms. "There was no brother. Maria's parents died early on, and she had no siblings."

"I'm sure your family believed that," Tom said. "But Maria once told Mrs. Brandenburg she had cut her brother off years earlier— for criminal behavior. And she hid that fact from just about everyone."

Miss Hutchinson fell silent for a few moments. She had known the Brandenburg family her entire life. "Oh, my goodness. I wonder why Maria never told my parents."

"Maybe she did," Pete suggested. "It's possible they didn't tell you."

"Possible, yes," she said. "But how do you know that . . . that she's the mystery writer, for sure?"

"One of her notebooks matches the handwriting of the treasure map," Tom spoke up, "*and* your letter."

"So she went into the water with Grant but escaped?"

"Yes, without a doubt. And Grant escaped too," Suzanne said. "But they seem to have fled the scene in opposite directions. Neither had any idea about the other's survival."

"Grant couldn't have even known that there *were* others," Pete said. "It's clear that the trauma of the accident and his near drowning had caused him to suffer from amnesia."

"Right up to the present," Suzanne said.

"What about the unfortunate woman, the skeleton?"

"No clue—yet," Tom replied.

"What was Maria doing out there?"

Kathy said, "It's our belief . . . that there was a romantic relationship."

Miss Hutchinson's face twisted. It was as if someone had struck her. "Oh, Lord. My father would have gone berserk."

"Which explains why Maria quit," Tom said.

"The police have arrested her brother?"

"Yes," Suzanne said. "He had moved into her home after his release from prison." She pulled her cell phone from her purse and hit *Play*. "Here's why they arrested him."

Miss Hutchinson watched the scene play out—the enraged man coming to the door, bat in hand, swinging, Kathy falling, Pete taking the hit before Tom came to the rescue.

Without warning, Miss Hutchinson's hand flew to her mouth. Her eyes remained locked on the screen as, breathing hard, she began to tear up.

"Miss Hutchinson," Suzanne cried. "What's the matter? What's wrong?"

"It's the kidnapper," she whispered. "The same man. I can tell by his movements . . . and his facial expression. He tried to grab me, twice. And you're telling me he—he was Maria's brother?"

20

HOMECOMING

G rant Dorrance Hutchinson—aka Sam Fellow—his wife, Claudia, and their daughter, Meryl, landed at Prescott Municipal Airport at 5:18 p.m. on Monday on a United Airlines flight that had departed Los Angeles that morning, with a stop in Phoenix. He was, the mystery searchers realized, about to experience the surprise of his life.

Now, as the aircraft taxied down the runway, it wasn't only Miss Hutchinson and the four young sleuths who were waiting for them. The story had been picked up by the wire services and gone national, as Chief Jackson had warned when the case began. A couple dozen reporters and photographers waited with the welcome party in Arrivals. Giant broadcast trucks from three television networks—poised to stream video footage worldwide—parked just outside the terminal too.

Right in the center of the action, luxuriating in the moment, was the person who had broken the story: Heidi Hoover from *The Daily Pilot.*

"She's holding court," Kathy said, giggling.

Just then, someone shouted, "The plane's landed!"

Chief Jackson arranged a front-row seat for Miss Hutchinson, right next to the Arrivals door. Sarah, her loyal maid and good friend for decades, sat beside her. Miss Hutchinson stood up now— visibly apprehensive and excited at the same time. Behind her were the mystery searchers, their parents, and Sheriff McClennan.

And behind *them* churned the chaos of the media scrum, shouting and jostling.

The door opened. A minute later, a somewhat nervous-looking Grant Dorrance Hutchinson stepped out of the tunnel and into the waiting arms of his weeping sister. His family was right behind him. The noise level rose. Electronic flashes burst. Photographers fought for position. Reporters bellowed their questions: "What's it like to come back from the dead?" "Do you remember anything about your family?" "Will you walk the mining trail at Skull Valley once more?"

"My goodness," Miss Hutchinson said to her brother, catching her breath and staring hard at a face she hadn't seen for more than fifty years. "You are the spitting image of Dad."

PRESCOTT'S "STORY OF THE CENTURY" DOMINATED THE MORNING edition of *The Daily Pilot.* "Grant Dorrance Hutchinson returns!" screamed the front-page, bold-face headline, with a narrative that detailed the strange twists and turns of a mystery that had befuddled multiple law enforcement agencies for five decades. There was a picture of Grant and his family surrounding Daisy, the four of them gazing into the camera, radiating pure happiness. A subhead read, "Prescott welcomes home a missing son." Another pic showed the four friends, arm-in-arm, with the caption, "Mystery searchers celebrate."

For a change, Suzanne liked her photograph. "Looks just like me."

"You sure?" Tom said.

THE NEXT FEW DAYS PASSED IN A BLUR.

Sam Fellow and his family stayed at his sister's old Victorian mansion for the better part of a week. There was much to talk about —after all, they had to get to know one another. The only son turned out to be a very affable man with a serious streak.

"No wonder," Suzanne said after one daily visit. "Imagine starting your life at seventeen, without a clue what had happened earlier. You'd be a thinker too, that's for sure."

Grant—"Sam" to his wife and daughter—answered questions about his journey. "You bet I remember him," he said, recalling the Highway Patrol officer in Bakersfield. "He gave me a few bucks for food, and then I hitched a ride to L.A. One couple picked me up— Tom and Alice Robertson—they hated the thought of someone my age being out so late at night. Drove me all the way to Van Nuys. We got along well. When we arrived there, they offered to put me up in their guest house for a few months." He chuckled. "They pretty much figured out I needed help."

He smiled at the memory. "Nicest people ever. Tom was the executive director of the local community college. He tested me and got me into classes, and that's how I started my life again."

Claudia spoke up. "In fact, we met at the community college."

"Well, that's strange enough," Kathy exclaimed. "The only reason you two met was because of the accident and Grant's amnesia. What are the odds?"

Miss Hutchinson insisted on calling her brother Grant, but it wasn't an easy transition for the Fellow family. Claudia laughed. "I understand why, Daisy, but we've all known him as Sam for a *long* time."

The mystery searchers ended up using his given name, Grant. And Miss Hutchinson insisted her newfound friends call her Daisy —and *Aunt* Daisy, for her brand-new niece, a person she couldn't have imagined just a week earlier. Meryl was overjoyed to have a new aunt—her first. Claudia had been an only child.

"Do you realize this is my only living family?" Daisy asked in wonder, more than once.

"And you're my only sibling," Grant had replied. He had a quiet, respectful way of talking. "Quite a shock, after all these years. A nice one, I would add."

There was a lot of talk about their parents. "You look like Dad, but have many of mother's mannerisms," Daisy informed him.

"Like what?"

"Like the way you walk and talk. And your easy laugh. Your sense of humor comes right from Mom. But those piercing blue eyes are a gift from Dad."

His laughter bubbled up often too. The thought of driving a brand-new Super Bee around town—at seventeen years of age—tickled him to no end. "I'm sure I figured I was someone special, parading that beauty around town."

"You sure did," his sister replied. "You were full of yourself too. But you drove me to school and back every day, and it was fun."

"What kind of student was I?"

"You maintained a B-plus average. Mom and Dad were quite proud of you. But you *excelled* at sports. You were Prescott High's quarterback in your junior year and took the team to the quarterfinals in Phoenix. I was there!"

"*Seriously?*" He couldn't believe it. "Did we win?"

As the days slipped by, the mystery searchers unfolded the events of their investigations, step by step—beginning with a treasure map found in a most unlikely place, and the discovery of the submerged 1970 Dodge Super Bee. Not to mention the mysterious skeleton, still unidentified.

Grant and his sister talked about everything—grandparents, friends, neighbors, likes and dislikes . . . and even Maria. Grant tried hard to piece his past together, but without success. "So you think it was a romantic relationship?" he asked the girls one day.

"Well, when you look at the title of the treasure map," Kathy said. "It kind of gives things away, right?"

A copy of the map sat on an end table in Daisy's parlor. Grant stared at it again for the umpteenth time. "'My Treasure Map,'" he murmured, almost to himself.

"You're not kidding," Daisy said, chuckling out loud. "You had a lot of girlfriends and more after that Super Bee arrived. But I'll tell you what, if Dad had known you were hanging around with Maria, all 'h' would have broken out. In his day, the household staff was *way* below his station in life—or his only son's."

"He was always a good-looking guy," Claudia said, winking at her husband.

"It explains why Maria quit, doesn't it?" Pete said.

"Sure does," Tom said. "And a few months later, her brother tried kidnapping you, Daisy."

"Did Maria know?" asked Meryl.

"Not at first," Suzanne replied. "But after the second attempt, a forensic artist's image of the would-be kidnapper appeared in *The Daily Pilot*. We think she put two and two together. By then she had cut all communication with her brother. It took her dying to open the door again, right after her brother's release from prison."

"When he moved into her house," Kathy said.

"What happens to him now?"

"The Chief says he violated the terms of his parole," Tom explained, "so he's going back to Arizona State Prison for a few years. Plus they've charged him with aggravated assault with a deadly weapon for whacking Pete, plus attempted murder for shooting at us in the desert. We won't ever see him again."

"Thank God," Daisy said grimly. "The police can't charge him with attempted kidnapping. Arizona's statute of limitations made sure of that. Still, I'm free now. I no longer fear an unknown attacker. It's a wonderful feeling."

Sarah walked in, bringing more coffee. "And about time too."

———

ONE DAY, GRANT AND HIS FAMILY WANDERED DOWN THE STREET TO the old homestead. The people living there welcomed him—by then his story had rocked all of Prescott—and provided a tour of the house, including his old bedroom. He remembered nothing.

He expressed an interest in visiting the pond. A large group made the trip, including the foursome. Claudia and Meryl tagged along too. It took three vehicles to drive the whole party out to Copper Basin Road. The hike in was quiet and respectful; everyone felt touched. Soon, a subdued Grant stood at the edge of the water, one hand shielding his eyes from the burning overhead sun. Claudia grasped his other hand as he focused on the north side, where the roadbed climbed out of the murkiness, up the ravine, and into the desert—right where his new life had begun.

"I remember the path," he murmured to his wife, pointing the way north. "And nothing else."

He wanted to see the Dodge Super Bee too. "There isn't much left," Suzanne warned, "except a rusted hulk." The girls drove him to the impound lot. Grant touched the steering wheel before backing away. They returned to the house on Brody Street.

It was late in the afternoon and the summer heat had dissipated. Soon enough, Grant and his family would head home to California.

The mysteries of Skull Valley had all come to the surface with one exception: the identity of the skeleton—the young lady with no name—remained an elusive secret.

21

A HERO EMERGES

The Fellow family was upstairs packing when Sheriff McClennan and Chief Jackson walked up and rang the doorbell.

"Huh," the Chief muttered. "I don't think it works." He hammered on the front door.

Sarah answered. She had met the two officers at the airport a few days earlier. "Sorry. Now that Miss Hutchinson feels safe again, we'll have that doorbell repaired. Please come in."

Minutes later, the foursome arrived with Heidi Hoover in tow. Everyone gathered in the parlor. Sarah pulled out a few folding chairs and offered lemonade.

"This is like a party," Daisy said as she strolled in, her face radiant.

"Yes," the sheriff said, "and a wake too. We have things to share with you."

"Uh-oh," Daisy said as she sat down. "Please, go ahead."

"Chuck Rodriquez has been talking," the Chief said. "And he has shed a little light on the case."

"We agreed to drop the attempted murder charge," the sheriff explained, "in exchange for his cooperation."

"He knew about the Skull Valley accident," the Chief said. "After Grant disappeared, a frightened and distraught Maria reconnected with him to seek his advice. He told her to shut her mouth and get out of the Hutchinsons' house. Months later, he tried to kidnap you, Miss Hutchinson." His eyes ticked over to her. "And the next year he made another attempt. Somehow, Maria figured out that he was the assailant—maybe from the newspaper description. But even before that event, she had zero contact with him for a whole year."

The sheriff cut in. "It was all about money, Miss Hutchinson. He figured if your family would pay fifty grand for a dead son, they'd happily pay a hundred grand for a live daughter."

Daisy's mouth moved, but no words came out.

"Decades passed with no communication between them," the sheriff continued, "until Chuck reconnected with Maria after his release from prison. She was dying and decided to forgive and forget. After she died, he cleaned her house out and dumped those books off at the thrift store. That was a mistake, but it fulfilled a promise Chuck had made to his sister. He felt safe loading them onto the dock at four in the morning—no way would anyone connect him with Maria. And the thought of a treasure map tucked into a book never crossed his mind. Then he read the story in *The Daily Pilot* . . . thanks to you, Heidi." He glanced over and caught her eye.

Heidi was scribbling madly but eked out a coy smile. "Always happy to help the local constabulary, sir."

"Well, that scared Chuck, big time," the Chief picked up the thread. "He worried that our four 'mystery searchers' here—or the police—would make their way to his door . . . uh, Maria's door, as it happened. That's why he freaked out when you all showed up. The possibility that his attempted-kidnapping escapades from so long ago might bubble to the top concerned him. *That's* why he fired at you in the desert."

"Geez," Pete said. "He tried to scare us off, but that led us right to him. Funny how things worked out."

"You bet," the Chief said. "Now we get to the identity of the young girl in the car. Her name was—is—Angela Muller. She was an *au pair* from Germany."

"An *au pair*," Meryl repeated. "Isn't that a woman who helps with housework or childcare—?"

"In exchange for room and board?" Kathy added.

"That's right—she was from Hamburg, Germany. No family, which is one reason she bonded with Maria. The two met at Prescott's Courthouse Plaza on Fourth of July prior to the accident and became instant friends."

Suzanne couldn't believe it. "She died a *month* later."

Daisy found her voice again. "What household did she serve? And why wasn't she reported missing?"

"That's the thing," the Chief replied. "She wasn't in service in Prescott—she lived with a family in Phoenix at the time of her disappearance."

"No wonder we couldn't find any trace of her," Tom said.

"Yeah, Phoenix City Police listed her as missing, but it appears the word didn't reach us."

"Isn't that crazy?" Daisy asked. "Wouldn't police forces have shared information?"

"Things were different back then," the sheriff responded, deflecting the jab. He had heard it all before. "The whole state was looking for Grant, but Angela didn't have a family—just a childcare position. Her employers reported her missing, but with no clues, the case went cold."

"Angela Muller," Kathy said, repeating her name. "How sad. But at least we can finally give her a decent burial."

"For sure," Suzanne said. "We'll find her a plot at Cemetery Hill."

"Well, we'll try to identify any living next of kin in Germany first. The other interesting thing is," the sheriff continued, glancing over at Grant, "you weren't driving the car at the time of the accident, sir. Angela was."

Grant sat up, shocked. "I was a passenger?"

"Yes. Angela drove, Maria sat in the center of the front seat, and you were to her right. You had leaned over and kissed Maria when Angela plunged the Dodge into the water."

"Sam!" Claudia cried as her husband turned beet red. Meryl stifled a smile with her hand.

"Boy, that must have been a heck of a kiss," Kathy whispered to Suzanne.

"See, Grant, what did I tell you?" Daisy taunted her brother. "You had *way* too many girlfriends. Little did the family realize that one of them was Maria. Had our father known . . ."

"Seatbelts were rare back then," the sheriff said, "It appears the two of you slammed into the front windshield hard. Maria told Chuck her head hurt for days."

"There's more," the Chief said, turning to Grant again. "She informed her brother that you saved her life. Somehow, you both escaped from the vehicle—from the driver's side window. Angela had somehow flipped into the back seat. Maria swallowed a lot of water, but you dragged her up to the old mining track. The last thing she remembered was you shouting, 'I'm going back for Angela!' before she passed out. Later, when she came to, wet and freezing cold, you were nowhere around. She waited, but neither you nor Angela ever appeared. She feared the worst and walked to Copper Basin Road. Then she hitchhiked home. The rest is history."

The final pieces of the puzzle had dropped into place. "So Maria headed south, but you made it to the *other* side of the pond . . . and hiked north," Tom said.

"I don't remember a thing about it," Grant said. "But I can see that darkened road in the desert like it was yesterday. Why were we driving out there?"

"Chuck told us that you and Maria had taken frequent trips around the old silver mines—that's where your family's fortune came from. It was one of your favorite places to drive. Angela arrived on her weekend off, and the three of you toured around together. You were showing her the sights."

"With a little romance on the side," Kathy joked.

The Chief stood up and held his hand out to Grant. "You're a hero, sir, and I don't meet many of them."

This time, Grant blushed as everyone gathered around him. He had one final question. "Why didn't Maria go to the police? Was it just because she was terrified of my father?"

"She was terrified of being *blamed*," the Chief replied. "She was the only survivor—who was to say that she wasn't driving the car, and recklessly too? She knew your father would seek retribution, and it scared her to death. So she accepted her brother's advice and moved. He told us the accident bothered her conscience every day of her life."

"That is so sad," Kathy said.

An hour later, the meeting ended. Everyone left, one at a time. Heidi rushed away with a new story for the morning edition. "People love hero stories," she said, as she often had before. And this was a great one.

The mystery searchers said their goodbyes. Daisy and Grant thanked each of them.

"Without you, none of this would have happened," Grant said. "You've given me back my past."

"And restored our family," Daisy said with a tear in her eye. "I'm free again—that horrible man is behind bars."

Grant said, "I'm sorry the reward expired."

"Me too," Pete said, rolling his eyes.

"Oh, *you* are our reward," Kathy said, giving them both a big hug. "This will always be our favorite mystery."

Claudia teared up while Meryl reveled in her parents' happiness. It had been quite a week for her too.

"Meryl, you have a special name," Suzanne said.

Tom nodded his head. "When you called and mentioned your first name, we knew our search for your father was over."

"I know it," Meryl replied, "I'd give anything to have met my grandmother."

On the way out to the car, Kathy received a text message. "Oh, wow, check this out. Who's this guy?"

The text read: *There are pirates operating out here and they're dangerous. I can't prove it but I need your help. Please call asap – Beau Bradley.*

Suzanne's eyes opened wide. "*What* is that all about?"

"You ever hear of the guy?" Tom asked, glancing at Kathy.

"Never."

"Another mystery!" Pete said, chortling. "Let's call him, now... *but wait*. First we need food."

EXCERPT FROM BOOK 6

THE VANISHING AT DECEPTION GAP

1
Pursuit

Suzanne lay flat atop a steel-bodied boxcar, insulated from the cold metal by a light jacket, jeans, and runners, stomach down and churning, her eyes peeking over the rim as she gasped for breath. Her heart thumped and even in the chilly early morning—it was after one a.m. in mid-August—she felt clammy and hot. Sweat poured out of her, soaking her forehead and staining her clothes. A welcome refreshing breeze sprang up, passing over and around her before dying away.

Something her father, Edward Jackson, often said—*Chief Edward Jackson of the Prescott City Police, that is*—popped into her mind. "Stick to it, like chewing gum on the sidewalk. Never give up." The thought forced a weak smile. *I am, Dad. And I won't.*

From her vantage point, snaking out in front were dozens of darkened boxcars, all in a stationary line, harnessed together and prepared for the morning journey out of Deception Gap Railroad Yards. The train would depart at daybreak, on the way to Denver with a two-hour layover in Cheyenne, Wyoming, loaded with freight from the Far East. Valuable freight.

There wasn't much to see: the line of boxcars faded into inky blackness. Not surprising, really: the railyard lights—capable of lighting up hundreds of acres with a flip of a switch that turned night into day—had shut down an hour earlier. Ahead of her, at the front of the line, sat two giant locomotives in the lead position. The mystery searchers had passed them earlier—huge, steel beasts ready to roll with ninety-some railcars extending northward before twisting at a soft, north-eastern angle.

The boxcar Suzanne hugged was at the end of the line—*Dead last,* she thought with a grimace, fully grasping the irony.

Fearful and cautious, she didn't dare move a muscle. No telling how close *they* were but her mind all but screamed: *What happened to Kathy? Did the boys escape? Where are those evil men?* And, moments later: *What was that sound?* Thankfully, the sound faded away but there were no other answers. Not yet. Just unnerving silence as her imagination raced at full tilt.

To the east was a dark view hidden by the next boxcar in line. Suzanne raised herself a foot higher to get above it, but there wasn't anything visible in the night. She knew the area was prairie flat and wide open: nothing but individual sets of steel tracks, one endless set after the other, with nowhere to hide. Not even a good-sized rock until the next hill emerged, right where Deception Gap ended.

To her left—to the northwest a few hundred yards away—was the immense, four-story, circular roundhouse, a relic from another century. Articulated by yellow light streaming through dirt-and-grime covered glass panes, the six-foot high windows surely hadn't seen a wet rag in years. The monster building operated twenty-four seven, every hour or two belching out smoke into a starry night, and capable—they were told—of servicing multiple locomotives at a time. Every so often, the *bang, bang, bang* of steel hammering steel penetrated the stillness.

Easy to get lost in *there* too. They discovered that on a previous foray. The hard way.

Bordering the roundhouse, close to the first set of tracks, appeared the three-story operations tower, dark and lonely—it closed down two hours earlier—together with smaller, non-descript structures, a dozen or more. Two or three warehouses, a variety of tool sheds, one foundry, four buildings untouched for decades … mostly one-story structures made of stone, well over a hundred years old. Chained and locked. *But not all,* Suzanne knew. Not all.

In the melee that had occurred minutes earlier, Tom and his best friend Pete Brunelli had simply vanished. Suzanne assumed they had raced eastwards, their only avenue of escape after the shocking attack: a gang of masked men, at least seven or eight she thought, had materialized from nowhere, screaming at the mystery searchers, cursing and swinging metal bars, dividing the foursome. The two girls—they had been trailing the boys—bolted in the only open direction, north-west, high-tailing it as fast as humanly possible.

Moments later, Kathy tripped, perhaps on one of those awful tracks or a wooden railway tie. Or maybe a pursuer grabbed her. *Who knows?* Either way, as she tumbled down, Kathy screamed, "Run, SUZIE, *RUN!*"

Suzanne did, as if the devil himself was after her. She stayed ahead of a handful of pursuers, hopping between boxcars, rolling under one to the other side before racing away without ever looking back until—

She glanced over her shoulder. Silence had descended behind her. The only sounds were her falling footsteps and heaving breathing—her own. Her pursuers appeared to have given up the chase. Gone. *Or had they?* She reached the end of the line and scrambled straight up a boxcar ladder before dropping onto its flat roof, blanketing herself against the steel top, trying desperately to control her rasping breath and still her beating heart.

Mixed emotions flooded her mind—fear, worry, uncertainty. Her old adversary, anger, had flared up too. *Not—liking—this,* she thought, her blood boiling as she replayed the scene of a swinging bar of steel that came her way. How it missed her was a mystery; she heard it wing by with a *whoosh*. She shuddered, attempting to regain control of herself, and heaved another deep breath. Then she reached for her cell phone in her jeans' back pocket.

It's not there! She groaned out loud. *Oh, Lord. It must have fallen out as I ran. Now what?*

She inched back to the ladder and glanced down: thirteen feet from the top of the boxcar to ground level, they had learned. Impossible to see anything in the dark. *Nothing.* She hesitated, more worried than before—as if that was even possible. A sudden light flashed from the ground below, twenty feet further up the track. *My phone! On mute, thank God.* Someone was calling. *Kathy!*

She flung her legs over the side and slid down the ladder, paying no heed to the danger. She raced over to her cell phone, her heart bursting with joy. But it wasn't Kathy—*Tom Jackson*, the screen read, with the stock close-up of her twin brother's smiling face. He never looked so good. She grabbed the cell and ducked under the boxcar, hiding behind its giant wheels.

"Tom, where *are* you?" she answered in a hoarse whisper.

Her brother's anxious relief poured out. "*Suzie!* We've been calling you. We made it to the locomotives. Are you both okay?"

"I am, but they caught Kathy."

Kathy's brother, Pete—his voice rising in the background with alarm—blurted, "*What?* You gotta be kidding! *They grabbed Kathy?*"

"She tripped or something and yelled at me to keep going. I outran them."

Tom thought of what his father would say. It wouldn't be pleasant. "Where are you now?"

"I'm hiding under the last boxcar. Those horrible criminals can't be far away." She hesitated. "What would they do with Kathy?"

Tom's mind raced. "Let's meet half-way, on the east side of the boxcars."

"Okay."

"Don't get caught," Pete warned. "That's the last thing we need."

"I hadn't planned on it," Suzanne retorted. She disconnected and poked her head out. All quiet. She rolled away and stood, listening once more, before retracing her steps alongside the boxcars.

Meanwhile, the boys deserted the relative safety of the lead locomotive's cabin. They dropped to ground level and trekked alongside the boxcars—slow and steady, treading softly, watching and listening for the first hint of danger.

At one point, Pete broke the silence, whispering, "We gotta rescue Kathy and soon too. If we can't find her, we need to call for reinforcements."

"Agreed," Tom muttered. "But right now all we can do is keep going. Suzanne should be close."

Moments later, a man's voice drifted their way, hanging in the breeze for a few seconds. Laughter rang out softly. Two men. The boys slipped under a boxcar, waiting until the threat melted in the distance. A loud banging sound started up, a hammering noise that droned relentlessly.

"From the roundhouse," Pete whispered as they continued their journey. By now, they figured Suzanne *had* to be getting close.

Then, without any warning, a woman screamed, a shattering wail that penetrated the night before cutting away half-way through.

"What the heck?" Pete blurted, grabbing Tom's arm and coming to a complete standstill. His hair stood straight up. "Was that …?"

They broke into a run.

Hi, fellow mystery searchers!
I hope you enjoyed this sneak peek at
The Vanishing at Deception Gap

Pick up a copy at your favorite retailer today!

And be sure to sign up for special deals and to hear about new book releases before anyone else. You can register here:

https://www.mysterysearchers.com/the-series/

BIOGRAPHY

Barry Forbes began his writing career in 1980, eventually scripting and producing hundreds of film and video corporate presentations, winning a handful of industry awards along the way. At the same time, he served as an editorial writer for Tribune Newspapers and wrote his first two books, both non-fiction.

In 1997, he founded and served as CEO for Sales Simplicity Software, a market leader which was sold two decades later.

What next? "I always loved mystery stories and one of my favorite places to visit was Prescott, Arizona. It's situated in rugged central Arizona with tremendous locales for mysteries." In 2017, Barry merged his interest in mystery and his skills in writing, adding in a large dollop of technology. The Mystery Searchers Family Book Series was born.

Barry's wife, Linda, passed in 2019 and the series is dedicated to her. "Linda proofed the initial drafts of each book and acted as my chief advisor." The couple had been married for 49 years and had two children. A number of their fifteen grandchildren provided feedback on each book.

Contact Barry: barry@mysterysearchers.com

ALSO BY BARRY FORBES

Book 1: The Mystery on Apache Canyon Drive

A small child wanders across a busy Arizona highway! In a hair-raising rescue, sixteen-year old twins Tom and Suzanne Jackson save the little girl from almost certain death. Soon, the brother and sister team up with best friends Kathy and Pete Brunelli on a perilous search for the child's past. The mystery deepens as one becomes two, forcing the deployment of secretive technology tools along Apache Canyon Drive. The danger level ramps up with the action, and the "mystery searchers" are born.

Book 2: The Ghost in the County Courthouse

A mysterious "ghost" bypasses the security system of Yavapai Courthouse Museum and makes off with four of the museum's most precious Native American relics. The mystery searchers, at the invitation of curator Dr. William Wasson, jump into the case and deploy a range of technology tools to discover the ghost's secrets. If the ghost strikes again, the museum's very future is in doubt. A dangerous game of cat and mouse ensues.

Book 3: The Secrets of the Mysterious Mansion

Heidi Hoover, a good friend and newspaper reporter for *The Daily Pilot*, introduces the mystery searchers to a mysterious mansion in the forest—at midnight! The mansion is under siege from unknown "hunters." *Who are they? What are they searching for?* Good, old-fashioned detective work and a couple of technology tools ultimately reveal the truth. A desperate race ensues, but time is running out.

Book 4: The House on Cemetery Hill

There's a dead man walking and it's up to the mystery searchers to figure out "why." That's the challenge from Mrs. Leslie McPherson, a successful but eccentric Prescott businesswoman. The mystery searchers team up with their favorite detective and utilize technology to spy on high-tech criminals at Cemetery Hill. It's a perilous game with heart-stopping moments.

Book 5: The Treasure of Skull Valley

Suzanne discovers a map hidden in the pages of a classic old book at the thrift store. It's titled "My Treasure Map" and leads past Skull Valley, twenty miles west of Prescott and into the high desert country—to an unexpected, shocking and elusive treasure. "Please help," the note begs. The mystery searchers utilize the power and reach of the Internet to trace the movement of people and events. . . half a century earlier.

Book 6: The Vanishing in Deception Gap

A text message to Kathy sets off a race into the unknown. "There are pirates operating out here and they're dangerous. I can't prove it, but I need your help." Who sent the message? Out where? Pirates! How weird is that? The mystery searchers dive in, but it might be too late. *The man has vanished into thin air.*

Book 7: The Heist Forgotten by Time

Coming – Fall/Winter, 2020

Don't forget to check out
www.MysterySearchers.com

Register to receive *free* parent/reader study guides for each book in the series—valuable teaching and learning tools for middle-grade students and their parents.

You'll also find a wealth of information on the website: stills and video scenes of Prescott, reviews, press releases, awards, and more. Plus, I'll update you on new book releases and other news.

Made in the USA
Monee, IL
06 September 2021